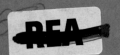

STARS OF THE
NEW CURFEW

STARS OF THE
NEW CURFEW

Ben Okri

VIKING

VIKING
Published by the Penguin Group
Viking Penguin, a division of Penguin Books USA Inc.,
40 West 23rd Street, New York, New York 10010, U.S.A.
Penguin Books Ltd, 27 Wrights Lane,
London W8 5TZ, England
Penguin Books Australia Ltd, Ringwood,
Victoria, Australia
Penguin Books Canada Ltd, 2801 John Street,
Markham, Ontario, Canada L3R 1B4
Penguin Books (N.Z.) Ltd, 182–190 Wairau Road,
Auckland 10, New Zealand

Penguin Books Ltd, Registered Offices:
Harmondsworth, Middlesex, England

First American Edition
Published in 1989 by Viking Penguin,
a division of Penguin Books USA Inc.

1 3 5 7 9 10 8 6 4 2

Library of Congress Cataloging in Publication Data
Okri, Ben.
Stars of the new curfew/Ben Okri.
p. cm.
ISBN 0-670-82520-4
I. Title.
PR9387.9.0394DS7 1989
823—dc19   88-40406
CIP

Printed in the United States of America
Set in Palatino

CONTENTS

We carry in our worlds that flourish
our worlds that have failed

Christopher Okigbo

In the Shadow of War

THAT AFTERNOON THREE soldiers came to the village. They scattered the goats and chickens. They went to the palm-frond bar and ordered a calabash of palm-wine. They drank amidst the flies.

Omovo watched them from the window as he waited for his father to go out. They both listened to the radio. His father had bought the old Grundig cheaply from a family that had to escape the city when the war broke out. He had covered the radio with a white cloth and made it look like a household fetish. They listened to the news of bombings and air raids in the interior of the country. His father combed his hair, parted it carefully, and slapped some aftershave on his unshaven face. Then he struggled into the shabby coat that he had long outgrown.

Omovo stared out of the window, irritated with his father. At that hour, for the past seven days, a strange woman with a black veil over her head had been going

3

past the house. She went up the village paths, crossed the Express road, and disappeared into the forest. Omovo waited for her to appear.

The main news was over. The radio announcer said an eclipse of the moon was expected that night. Omovo's father wiped the sweat off his face with his palm and said, with some bitterness:

'As if an eclipse will stop this war.'

'What is an eclipse?' Omovo asked.

'That's when the world goes dark and strange things happen.'

'Like what?'

His father lit a cigarette.

'The dead start to walk about and sing. So don't stay out late, eh.'

Omovo nodded.

'Heclipses hate children. They eat them.'

Omovo didn't believe him. His father smiled, gave Omovo his ten kobo allowance, and said:

'Turn off the radio. It's bad for a child to listen to news of war.'

Omovo turned it off. His father poured a libation at the doorway and then prayed to his ancestors. When he had finished he picked up his briefcase and strutted out briskly. Omovo watched him as he threaded his way up the path to the bus-stop at the main road. When a danfo bus came, and his father went with it, Omovo turned the radio back on. He sat on the window-sill and waited for the woman. The last time he saw her she had glided past with agitated flutters of her yellow smock. The children stopped what they were doing and stared at her. They had said that she had no shadow. They had said that her feet never touched the ground. As she went past, the children began to throw things at her. She didn't flinch, didn't quicken her pace, and didn't look back.

The heat was stupefying. Noises dimmed and lost their edges. The villagers stumbled about their various tasks as if they were sleep-walking. The three soldiers drank palm-wine and played draughts beneath the sun's oppressive glare. Omovo noticed that whenever children went past the bar the soldiers called them, talked to them, and gave them some money. Omovo ran down the stairs and slowly walked past the bar. The soldiers stared at him. On his way back one of them called him.

'What's your name' he asked.

Omovo hesitated, smiled mischievously, and said:

'Heclipse.'

The soldier laughed, spraying Omovo's face with spit. He had a face crowded with veins. His companions seemed uninterested. They swiped flies and concentrated on their game. Their guns were on the table. Omovo noticed that they had numbers on them. The man said:

'Did your father give you that name because you have big lips?'

His companions looked at Omovo and laughed. Omovo nodded.

'You are a good boy,' the man said. He paused. Then he asked, in a different voice:

'Have you seen that woman who covers her face with a black cloth?'

'No.'

The man gave Omovo ten kobo and said:

'She is a spy. She helps our enemies. If you see her come and tell us at once, you hear?'

Omovo refused the money and went back upstairs. He re-positioned himself on the window-sill. The soldiers occasionally looked at him. The heat got to him and soon he fell asleep in a sitting position. The cocks, crowing dispiritedly, woke him up. He could feel the afternoon softening into evening. The soldiers dozed in the bar. The hourly news came on. Omovo listened without comprehension to the day's casualties. The announcer succumbed to the stupor, yawned, apologized, and gave further details of the fighting.

Omovo looked up and saw that the woman had already gone past. The men had left the bar. He saw them weaving between the eaves of the thatch houses, stumbling through the heat-mists. The woman was further up the path. Omovo ran downstairs and followed the men. One of them had taken off his uniform top. The soldier behind had buttocks so big they had begun to split his pants. Omovo followed them across the Express road. When they got into the forest the men stopped following the woman, and took a different route. They seemed to know what they were doing. Omovo hurried to keep the woman in view.

He followed her through the dense vegetation. She wore faded wrappers and a grey shawl, with the black veil covering her face. She had a red basket on her head. He completely forgot to determine if she had a shadow, or whether her feet touched the ground.

He passed unfinished estates, with their flaking

ostentatious signboards and their collapsing fences. He passed an empty cement factory: blocks lay crumbled in heaps and the workers' sheds were deserted. He passed a baobab tree, under which was the intact skeleton of a large animal. A snake dropped from a branch and slithered through the undergrowth. In the distance, over the cliff edge, he heard loud music and people singing war slogans above the noise.

He followed the woman till they came to a rough camp on the plain below. Shadowy figures moved about in the half-light of the cave. The woman went to them. The figures surrounded her and touched her and led her into the cave. He heard their weary voices thanking her. When the woman reappeared she was without the basket. Children with kwashiorkor stomachs and women wearing rags led her half-way up the hill. Then, reluctantly, touching her as if they might not see her again, they went back.

He followed her till they came to a muddied river. She moved as if an invisible force were trying to blow her away. Omovo saw capsized canoes and trailing water-logged clothes on the dark water. He saw floating items of sacrifice: loaves of bread in polythene wrappings, gourds of food, Coca-Cola cans. When he looked at the canoes again they had changed into the shapes of swollen dead animals. He saw outdated currencies on the riverbank. He noticed the terrible smell in the air. Then he heard the sound of heavy breathing from behind him, then someone coughing and spitting. He recognized the voice of one of the soldiers urging the others to move faster. Omovo crouched in the shadow of a tree. The soldiers strode past. Not long afterwards he heard a scream. The men had caught up with the woman. They crowded round her.

'Where are the others?' shouted one of them.

The woman was silent.

'You dis witch! You want to die, eh? Where are they?'

She stayed silent. Her head was bowed. One of the soldiers coughed and spat towards the river.

'Talk! Talk!' he said, slapping her.

The fat soldier tore off her veil and threw it to the ground. She bent down to pick it up and stopped in the attitude of kneeling, her head still bowed. Her head was bald, and disfigured with a deep corrugation. There was a livid gash along the side of her face. The bare-chested soldier pushed her. She fell on her face and lay still. The lights changed over the forest and for the first time Omovo saw that the dead animals on the river were in fact the corpses of grown men. Their bodies were tangled with river-weed and their eyes were bloated. Before he could react, he heard another scream. The woman was getting up, with the veil in her hand. She turned to the fat soldier, drew herself to her fullest height, and spat in his face. Waving the veil in the air, she began to howl dementedly. The two other soldiers backed away. The fat soldier wiped his face and lifted the gun to the level of her stomach. A moment before Omovo heard the shot a violent beating of wings just above him scared him from his hiding place. He ran through the forest screaming. The soldiers tramped after him. He ran through a mist which seemed to have risen from the rocks. As he ran he saw an owl staring at him from a canopy of leaves. He tripped over the roots of a tree and blacked out when his head hit the ground.

When he woke up it was very dark. He waved his fingers in front of his face and saw nothing. Mistaking the darkness for blindness he screamed, thrashed around, and ran into a door. When he recovered from his shock he heard voices outside and the radio crackling on about the war. He found his way to the balcony, full of wonder that his sight had returned. But when he got there he was surprised to find his father sitting on the sunken cane chair, drinking palm-wine with the three soldiers. Omovo rushed to his father and pointed frantically at the three men.

'You must thank them,' his father said. 'They brought you back from the forest.'

Omovo, overcome with delirium, began to tell his father what he had seen. But his father, smiling apologetically at the soldiers, picked up his son and carried him off to bed.

Worlds That Flourish

I was at work one day when a man came up to me and asked me my name. For some reason I couldn't tell it to him immediately and he didn't wait for me to get around to it before he turned and walked away. At lunch-time I went to the bukka to eat. When I got back to my desk someone came and told me that half the workers in the department had been sacked. I was one of them.

I had not been working long in the department and I left the job without bitterness. I packed my things that day and sorted out the money that was owed me. I got into my battered little car and drove home. When I arrived I parked my car three streets from where I lived, because the roads were bad. As I walked home the sight of tenements and zinc huts made me dizzy. Swirls of dust came at me from the untarred roads. Everything shimmered like mirages in an omnipotent heat.

Later in the evening I went out to buy some cooked food. On my way back a neighbour came to me and said:

'How are you?'

'Fine,' I said.

'Are you sure you are fine?'

'Yes. Why do you ask?'

'Well,' said the neighbour, 'it's because you go around as if you don't have any eyes.'

'What do you mean?'

'Since your wife died you've stopped using your eyes. Haven't you noticed that most of the compound people are gone?'

'Gone where?'

'Run away. To safety.'

'Why?'

'Don't ask me.'

'Why haven't you gone?'

'I'm happy here.'

'So am I,' I said, smiling. I went to my room.

Barely two hours after the conversation with my neighbour there was a knock on my door. I opened it and three men pushed their way in. Two of them carried machetes and the third had a gun. They weren't nasty or brutal. They merely asked me to sit quietly on the bed and invited me to watch them if I wanted. I watched them as they cleaned my room of my important possessions and took what money they could find. They chatted to me about how bad the roads were and how terrible the government was and how there were so many checkpoints around. While they chatted they bundled my things into a heap and carried them out to their lorry as though they were merely helping me to move. When they finished the man with the gun said:

'This is what we call scientific robbery. If you so much as cough after we've gone I will shoot out your eyes, you hear?'

I nodded. He left with a smile. A moment later I heard their lorry driving off down the untarred road. I rushed out and they were gone. I came back to my room to decide what next to do. I couldn't inform the police immediately because the nearest station was miles away and even if I did I couldn't really expect them to do anything. I sat on the bed and tried to convince myself that I was quite fortunate to still have the car and some money in the bank. But as it turned out I wasn't even allowed to feel fortunate. Not long after the thieves had left there was another knock on my door. I got up to open it when five soldiers with machine-guns stepped into the room. Apparently the thieves had been unable to get away. They were stopped at a checkpoint and to save their own necks they told the soldiers that I was their accomplice. Without ceremony, and with a great deal of roughness, the soldiers dragged me to their jeep. Visions of being executed as an armed robber at the beach filled me with vertigo. I told the soldiers that I was the one who was robbed but the soldiers began to beat me because it seemed to them I was trying to insult their intelligence with such a transparent lie. As they took me away, with their guns prodding my back, my neighbour came out of his room. When he saw the soldiers with me he said:

'I told you that you don't have eyes.'

Then he went to one of the soldiers and, to my astonishment, said:

15

'Mr Soldier, I hope you treat him as he deserves. I always thought something was wrong with his head.'

The soldiers took us to the nearest police station and we were all locked in the same cell. The real thieves, who seemed to find it all amusing, kept smiling at me. At night the soldiers came and beat us up with whips when we refused to confess anything. Then in the morning some policemen took us outside and made us strip naked and commanded us to face the street. The people that went past looked at us and hurried on. I shouted of my innocence and the policemen told me to shut up. We stayed out facing the whole world in our nakedness for most of the day. The children laughed at us. The women studied us. Photographers came and flashed their cameras in our eyes. When night fell a policeman came and offered me the opportunity to bribe my way out of trouble. I burned all over and my eyes were clogged with dust. I told him I had to go to the bank first. The thieves paid their dues and were freed. I stayed in a cell crammed with men screaming all night. In the morning one of the soldiers accompanied me to the bank. I drew out some money and paid my dues. I went home and slept for the rest of that day.

In the morning I went to have a shower. Going through the compound I was struck by the absence of communal noises. No music came from the rooms. No children cried. There were no married couples arguing and shouting behind red curtains. There were chickens and rats in the backyard. My neighbour came out of the toilet and smiled when he saw me.

16

'So they have released you,' he said, regretfully.

'You are a wicked man,' I shouted.

'People don't go out anymore,' he said, coolly ignoring me. 'It's very quiet. I like it this way.'

'Why were you so wicked to me?'

'I don't trust people who don't have eyes.'

'I might have been executed.'

'Are you better than those who have been?'

I stared at him in disbelief. He went and washed his hands at the pump and dried them against his trousers. He pushed past me and went to his room. A moment later I saw him going out.

I still felt sleepy even after my shower. I went to my room and got dressed. Then I went to the front of the compound. I sat on a bench and looked at the street. The churches around were not having their usual prayers and songs over loudspeakers. The muezzin was silent. The street was deserted. There were no signs of panic. The stalls still had their display of goods and the shops were open, but there was no one around. There were a lot of birds in the air, circling the aerials. Somewhere in the distance a radio had been left on. Across the street a goat wandered around the roots of a tree. The cocks didn't crow. After a while all I heard inside me was a confused droning, my incomprehension. Something had been creeping on us all along and now that the street was empty I couldn't even see what it was. I sat outside, fighting the mosquitoes, till it became dark. Then it dawned on me that something had happened to time. I seemed to be sitting in an empty space without history. The wind wasn't cooling. And then suddenly all the

17

lights went out. It was as if the spirit of the world had finally died. The black-out lasted a long time.

For many days I wandered about in the darkness of the city. I drove around in the day looking for jobs. Everywhere I went workers were being sacked in great numbers. There were no strikes. Sometimes I listened to the Head of State's broadcasts on the radio. He spoke about austerity, about tightening the national belt, and about a great future. He sounded very lonely, as though he were talking in a vast and empty room. After his broadcasts music was played. The music sounded also as if it were played in an empty space.

In the evenings I went around looking for friends. They had gone and no explanations or forwarding addresses were given. When I went to their compounds I was surprised at how things had changed. The decay of the compounds seemed to have accelerated. Doors were left open. Cobwebs hung over the compound fronts. Outside the house of a friend I saw a boy staring at me with frightened eyes. When I started to ask him of the whereabouts of my friend, he got up and ran. I went back to my car and drove around the city, looking for people that I knew. Then I really began to notice things. There were people scattered in places of the city. There seemed no panic on their faces. It began to occur to me that the world was emptying out. When I took a closer look at the people a strange thought came to me: they seemed like sleep-walkers. I stopped the car and went amongst them to get a closer look, to talk with them, and find out exactly what was happening. (The radios and newspapers had long stopped giving information.) I went out into the street and approached a woman who was frying yams at the roadside. She looked at me with burning, suspicious eyes.

'What is happening to the country?' I asked her.

'Nothing is happening.'

'Where has everyone gone?'

'No one has gone anywhere. Why are you asking me? Go and ask someone else.'

As I turned to go the fire flared up, illuminating her face. And on her face I saw a sloping handwriting. On her forehead and on her cheeks there were words. Then I noticed that her hands were also covered in handwriting. I drew closer to read the words, but she began screaming. I heard the ironclad boots of soldiers running down the streets towards us. I hurried to my car and drove off.

As I went home I noticed that a lot of the people in the streets had handwriting on their faces. I couldn't understand why I hadn't noticed it before. And then I was suddenly overcome with the notion that my neighbour had words on his face. I drove home hurriedly.

It was dark by the time I arrived. I couldn't risk having the car three streets away, so I parked it outside the compound. I think it was with that act of caution that the thought of fleeing first occurred to me. The birds had increased over our street. The radio was still on somewhere in the distance. Its battery was getting weaker. The wind whistled through the compounds. Stray dogs roamed down the street. I sat outside and waited for my neighbour. When he didn't come back for a long time I went and knocked on his door. There was no reply. I went to my room and ate, and then I went and sat outside again. I listened to the radio dying. I listened to the thin military voices. The night got darker and still my neighbour didn't return. I listened to the wind straining the branches of the trees. Stray cats eyed me in the dark. I went to my room and I slept that night with the feeling that something was breaking on my consciousness. When I woke up in the morning I noticed that the Head of State's lonely face kept slipping into my mind. I had a shower and ate and went and knocked on my neighbour's door. He still hadn't got back.

I prepared to go out but thunder sounded in the sky. By the afternoon it had started to rain. The street swelled with water. The gutters overran. The rain poured into the open doors of the rooms and fell on the stalls with their undisturbed display of goods and beat down on the clothes that had been left hanging. The wind blew very hard and shook our roof. The branches of a tree strained and then cracked. From afar I could see smoke above the houses. The rain poured down unceasingly for two days. My neighbour still didn't return. The water went up to the bumper of my car. The rain finally extinguished the distant radio. The Head of State made desperate broadcasts about cleaning the national stables. I sat in my room, imprisoned by the rain. I listened to the water endlessly falling. My roof began to leak. I heard a cat wailing above the steady din. Sometimes the rain accelerated in its fall, and managed to obliterate both time and memory. It soon seemed as if it had always been raining. With the city empty of people, I began to hear broadcasts in the rain. And then in the evening of the second day, a realization came upon me. I went to the window, my ears reverberating with persistently dripping water, and looked out. That was when I discovered I had temporarily lost the names of things.

I stayed indoors till the rain stopped. Then I stayed in another day, to enable the water to sink into the swollen earth. I went and tried my neighbour's door several times and then I went into his room. Nothing had been disturbed, but he seemed to have altogether vanished. On the fourth day I ventured down our street and witnessed the proliferation of disasters. Trees had fallen. Houses had crumbled before the force of the wind and rain. Dead cats floated in the gutters. There were no birds in the air. I went back to my room. My head jostled with signs. I got out my box and stuffed it full of my papers and clothes. I packed all my food into the back of the car. I left my door open. I tried my neighbour's room for the final time. I got into my car and set out on a journey without a destination through the vast, uncultivated country.

It wasn't easy getting out of the city. There were so many roadblocks and soldiers were all over the place. They stopped me and searched the car. At every one of the roadblocks the soldiers commented on the food I had at the back. They asked where I was going. I told them I was going to visit my mother who was ill in the village. Then they would ask if I thought that people were hungry. When I said no, the soldiers would take some of my food and wave me on. By the time I cleared through the last roadblock I had very little food left. But that wasn't what worried me. What made me anxious, as I drove through the forests, was that the car kept giving me trouble. It would stall and I had to sit at the wheel and wait for the engine to cool. When it did start, and move, it did so erratically. The car would suddenly, it seemed, start driving me. It picked up speed, and slowed down, of its own inscrutable volition.

I drove for a long time down the winding forest roads. I managed to cross a wooden bridge that had been partly devastated by rain. For long periods of time I heard only the purring sound of the car. Sometimes it seemed as if I were driving on one spot. The road and the forests didn't seem to change. I crossed the same partly devastated bridge several times. I got tired of driving without seeming to be moving. I stopped and locked all the doors and got some sleep.

I felt better when I woke up. I was driving for a while when I felt that I had broken the sameness of the journey. Mountain ranges, plateaus of ambergris rocks, and precipices, appeared all around me. I passed a clay-coloured anthill. I slowed down for a pack of hyenas to cross the road. I came to a petrol shack. The door was open. There were dirty barrels of petrol and diesel oil in the front yard. I stopped the car and parked. I passed the greasy hand-pump and knocked on the door. An old man came out. He had a pair of grey braces over a black shirt and he wore filthy khaki trousers. He was barefoot.

'You're the first person I've seen for a long time,' he said.

I asked him to fill the tank. He didn't say anything to

me as he did so. I changed the water in the radiator. He
didn't have any brake fluid. I sat on a bench and listened
to the insects of the forest while he slowly and pains-
takingly looked the car over and tuned the engine.

'How do you manage to live here?'

'I manage. I like it.'

I paid him. As I was getting into the car the old man
said:

'Don't go that way. I haven't seen any vehicles coming
back. Stay where you can be happy.'

I nodded, smiling. I shut the door and started the car.
As I moved away I waved at him. He didn't wave back.
He stared at the car motionlessly. I drove on into the
forest.

Further along I ran over a goat that had been crossing
the road. I felt the wheels bump over its body and I
stopped. The goat jerked on the tarmac. When I came out
of the car I heard violent noises and saw people emerging
from the forest and rushing towards me. The men had
machetes and the women held long pieces of firewood. I
ran back to the car, but when I started it the engine only
whined. The people pounced on the car and smashed
the bodywork with their machetes and firewood. They
broke the windows and several hands reached for my
face. The car started, suddenly, and I sped off with a few
hands still grasping for my eyes. I swerved both ways
and people fell off and I drove on without looking back.
Afterwards I saw blood and bits of flesh on the jagged,
broken windows.

And then it was as if the rain that had fallen in the city
began to catch up with me, intensified. The forest

23

reverberated with thunder. Lightning struck in the trees. The leaves were blown into frenzies by the relentless wind. The car kept swerving and sometimes it was as if the wind was blowing the car on, lifting it at the back. Sometimes I did not feel that the wheels were on the road. I drove on air. I drove on through the torrential rain. There were trees swaying and leaves flapping everywhere. And then there was water pouring on the trees everywhere. Now and again someone would emerge, soaking, from the forest and would run across the road and wave for me to stop. I did not stop for anybody, or for any reason. I drove on in demented concentration. Soon my eyes got tired. I was thrashed by the rain and all I could see was the windscreen and the forests distorted in the rain. I found it difficult to blink and when I did I felt the blankness pulling me into sleep. I would wake up to find myself veering off the road. I managed to sleep while driving.

When night came thickly over the forest I couldn't separate the darkness from the rain. Occasionally I saw a flash behind me which I thought belonged to a car. I adjusted the mirror and in the crack of a second I saw my face. Thunder broke and exploded in front of me. A moment later there was a forked, incandescent flash which lit up the handwriting on my face. I negotiated a bend and heard a deafening crash in the forest. Something shattered my windscreen and I drove wide-eyed into the darkness. Insects flew into my face. Wind, rain, and bits of glass momentarily blinded me. Then I saw that a tree had fallen across the road ahead of me. The car spun into the vortex of leaves and branches. And then there was stillness. For a long moment it was completely dark. I couldn't hear, see, or feel anything. And then I heard the whirring engine and the insistent din of insects and rain.

I tried to move, but couldn't: I felt I had become entangled in the car. I heard magnified grating noises. I was covered in crumbly earth which seemed alive and which stung me. Something settled inside me and I extricated myself from the front seat effortlessly. When I was out of the wreckage I saw that the car had run into a large anthill. There were ants everywhere. I pushed on through the rain. I couldn't find the road. I went on into the forest. I passed rocks flowering with lichen. I moved under the endless lattice of branches. Thorns of the forest cut into me. I didn't bleed.

I came to a river. When I swam across I noticed it was flowing in a direction opposite to how it seemed. As I came out on the other bank the water dried instantly on me. I went on through the undergrowth till I came to a village. At the entrance there were two palm trees growing upside down. I went between the trees and saw a man sitting on a chair outside a hut. When the man saw me his face lit up. He ululated suddenly and talking drums sounded at distances in the village. The man got up and rushed to me and embraced me:

'We've been waiting for you,' he said.

'What do you mean?'

'We've been waiting for you.'

'That can't be true.'

The man looked quite offended at my remark, but he said:

'I have been sitting outside this hut for three months. Waiting for you. I'm happy that you've made it. Come, the people of the village are expecting you.'

He led the way.

'Why?'

'You'll find out.'

I followed him silently. As we went on into the village, I noticed that there was a woman following us. Whenever I looked back she hid behind the trees and bushes.

'We've been cleaning up the village for your arrival,' the man said.

We passed a skyscraper that reflected the sunlight like blinding glass sheets.

'That's where the meeting will take place.'

The huts looked solid and clean with their white ochred walls. The iroko and baobab trees were neatly spaced. The bushes were lush. The air was scented with flamingo flowers.

We arrived at the village square when it occurred to me that the place was vaguely familiar. It was a very orderly and clean place. And then suddenly I realized that I couldn't see. I didn't hear the man leading me anymore. I heard singing and dancing all around. I panicked and started shouting. The dancing and singing stopped. I stood for a long time, casting about in the menacing silence. After a while, when I quietened down, I heard light footsteps coming towards me.

'Help me,' I said.

Then a woman, who smelt of cloves, in a sweet voice, said:

'Be quiet and follow me.'

I followed her till we came to a place that smelt of bark. She opened a door and we went in. She pulled up a stool for me. I could have been sitting on solid air for all I knew, but the woman's presence reassured me. I heard her moving about the place. She set down food for me. I ate. She set down drinks and I drank. Then she said:

'This will be your new home.'

Then I heard the door shut. I soon fell asleep.

When I woke up I felt things coming out of my ears. Things were crawling all over me. I stood up and called out. The door opened and the woman came in and led me to the place where I had a wash. After I had eaten, she sat near me and said:

'We heard you were coming. It took a long time.'

'How did you hear?'

'You will find out.'

'Why have you all been waiting for me?'

She was silent. Then she laughed and said:

'Didn't you know we have been waiting for you?'

'No.'

'Didn't you know you were coming here?'

'No. But why?'

'To take your place in the assembly.'

'What assembly?'

'We kept postponing the meeting because you hadn't arrived.'

I grew weary of asking questions.

27

'The people of the village have been anxious,' she said.
'When is this meeting taking place?'
'Two days' time.'
'Why not today?'
'The elders thought you needed time to rest and get used to the village. It's an important meeting.'
'What is the meeting about?'
'You are tired. Get some sleep. If you need me call.'
Then I heard the door open and shut again.

In the village everything had a voice and everything spoke at me. Sounds and voices assaulted me and my ears began to ache. Then slowly my sight returned. At first it was like seeing through milk. When my vision cleared, the voices stopped. Then I saw the village as I had not seen it before.

I went out of the place I was staying and walked around in bewilderment. Some of the people of the village had their feet facing backwards. I was amazed that they could walk. Some people came out of tree-trunks. Some had wings, but they couldn't fly. After a while I got used to the strangeness of the people. I ceased to really notice their three legs and elongated necks. What I couldn't get used to were the huts and houses that were walled round with mirrors on the outside. I didn't see myself reflected in them as I went past. Some people walked into the mirrors and disappeared. I couldn't walk into them.

After some time of moving around, I couldn't find my way back to where I stayed. I went about the village listening for the voice of the woman who had been taking care of me. I stopped at a communal water-pump and a woman came up to me and said:

'What are you doing here?'

'I'm lost.'

'I'll take you back.'

I followed her.

'So you can see now?' she asked, turning her head right round to me as she walked.

'Yes.'

And then I had the distinct and absurd feeling that I knew her. She was a robust figure, with a face of jagged and familiar beauty. She wore a single flowerprint wrapper and was barefoot. Her skin was covered in native chalk. Her eyes radiated a strange light which dazzled like a green mirror.

'Who are you?'

She didn't answer my question. When we got to an obeche tree she opened a door on the trunk. Inside I saw a perfect interior, neat and compact and warm.

'I'm not going in there,' I said.

She turned her head towards me, her face was expressionless.

'But this has been your new home,' she said.

'It can't be. It's too small.'

She laughed almost affectionately.

'When you come in you will find it is large enough.'

It was very spacious when I went in. I sat down on the wooden bed. She served me food in a half calabash. The rice seemed to move on the plate like several white maggots. I could have sworn it was covered in spider's webs. But it tasted sweet and was satisfying. The cup from which I was supposed to drink bled on the outside. After she had cleared the food from the table, I pretended to be asleep. Before she left I heard her say:

'Sleep well and regain your strength. The meeting is taking place tonight.'

I sat up.

'Who are you?' I asked.

She shut the door gently behind her.

I waited for some time before I got up and left the tree. I was intent on fleeing, but I didn't want to betray it. As I wandered round the village looking for the way out, I heard people dancing, I heard some disputing the village principles, I heard others reciting a long list of names, and I heard beautiful voices telling stories behind the trees. But I could not see any of the people.

And then as I passed a hut, from which came the high-pitched laughter of shy young girls, I noticed that a one-eyed goat was staring at me intently. I hurried on. Dogs and chickens gazed at me. I experienced the weird sensation that people were staring at me through the eyes of the animals. I passed the village shrine. In front of it there was the mighty statue of a god with big holes for eyes. I was convinced the god was spying on me.

I wandered for a long time looking for the exit. I heard disembodied voices saying that the big meeting would soon begin. The lights hadn't changed. I came to a frangipani tree full of white birds. Beyond the tree was the village square and beyond the square was the entrance. I pushed on till I came to the hut. Sitting on the chair outside the hut was a man who had three eyes on his face. He kept staring at me and I was forced to greet him.

'Don't greet me,' he said.

He went on staring at me, as though he expected me to recognize him. His three eyes puzzled and disorientated me. But when I concentrated on the two normal eyes I suddenly did recognize him. He was my vanished neighbour.

'What are you doing here?' I asked.

'What do you think?'

'I don't know.'

'A soldier shot me.'

'Shot you?' I asked, surprised.

'Yes.'

'Why?'

'To kill me. What are you doing here?'

'Me?'

'Yes.'

'I don't know.'

He laughed.

'They will tell you at the meeting.'

'What is the meeting about?'

'Life and death.'

'What life, what death?'

He laughed again, but more explosively. There was something about his mouth, the way his eyes moved, that gradually made things clear to me. I backed away in terror.

'You better not try and escape,' he said maliciously.

That was all I needed. I ran towards the entrance and things got scrambled up as I ran. And then I found that I was moving not forwards, but backwards. I passed the white ochred huts and the blinding skyscraper. I heard the high-pitched scream of a woman. Talking drums sounded in frenzies. When I stopped and ran backwards, I found I was actually running forwards. Then I saw the woman who had screamed, and for the first time I recognized her as my dead wife. She tore after me in great distress. Men and women and disembodied voices came after me with their wings that didn't help them fly and their feet which were turned backwards. I fled past the trees that were upside down and the cornfields outside the village entrance. The cornplumes were golden and beautiful. The people of the village pursued me all the way to the boundary.

I crossed the river. Birds came at me from the forest. I ran for a long time without stopping till I came to my car that had smashed through the branches of the tree and devastated the anthill. I am not sure what happened next but when I came to I found myself in the wreckage of the car. I was covered with ants and they bit me mercilessly. The twisted wreck of metal seemed to have grown on me and I could feel my blood drying on the seat. There were cuts and broken glass on my face. I spent a very long time struggling to get out of the car. When I did I felt about as wrecked as the car and my body felt like it had already died. I staggered through the forest. I ate lemon grass leaves. As I pushed my way through the forest I became aware that I could see spirits. It was morning before I could find the main road. After a while of stumbling down the road I saw a car coming towards me. I stuck out my hand and waved furiously and was surprised when the car stopped. There was a young man at the wheel. He wound down his side window and I said:

32

'Don't go that way. Find where you can be happy.'

But the young man looked me over, nodded, and drove straight on. I watched the car till it had disappeared. Then I trudged on with the hope of reaching the old man's shack before I died.

In the City of Red Dust

—◆—

For unto every one that hath shall be given, and he shall have abundance: but from him that hath not shall be taken away even that which he hath

Matthew 25:29

1

EMOKHAI WAS SITTING on the wall in front of the house when the aerial manoeuvres started. He was very broke and had made plans with his friend to go to the hospital and earn some money. He had gone to sleep on an empty stomach and he hadn't eaten that morning. His friend was late.

With his eyes dry, so that he had to keep blinking, Emokhai watched the military planes flying overhead. They made practice dives for the afternoon's parade. The planes crossed one another's paths and circled into formation. They stalled in the air, tumbled down as if they might crash into the teeming shacks below, then swooped back up into the sky with perfect rhythmic control. The inhabitants of the city marvelled at the displays. The children screamed excitedly. The women, palms to their breasts, exclaimed with breathless amazement. Emokhai was unimpressed.

It was the military governor's fiftieth birthday. The city bustled with an increased military presence. It was widely rumoured that the celebrations being planned would make this one the most memorable for years to come.

Emokhai jumped down from the wall. The heat was dry and the air powdered with ochre-dust. He went towards Mama Joe, who sold jollof rice in front of the house. She looked up at him:

'This governor of ours knows how to celebrate.'

'Don't mind him,' Emokhai replied.

They watched the planes. The dry heat preyed on him. A sudden stench of rotting eggs came from across the road. The planes dived, and the span of their wings cast swift giant shadows over the sprawling tenements.

'Can you borrow me another five naira?' he asked, as casually as possible.

Mama Joe sheltered her eyes and squinted at the thundering planes.

'What about the money you owe me already?'

'When Marjomi comes I will pay you.'

'That's what you always say.'

'What about some rice?'

She dished him a small portion on a green plastic plate. He ate ravenously, undisturbed by the odours of the street. When he finished he washed the plate, dried his hands, and said:

'I feel better already.'

He thanked Mama Joe and set out in search of his

friend. He had jumped over a gutter, and was lolling down the road littered with refuse, when he glimpsed the steel shadow of a diving plane. He ducked. When he looked up the plane, vibrating, had shot back up into the sky. Emokhai sneaked past the 'Good Samaritan' pools office, where he owed the manager some money, and crossed the busy road. On the other side a truck-pusher strained at an impossible load of yams. Emokhai moved on into the clean avenues that were named after rich men, governors, and freedom fighters. Then he went towards the tracts of forest on the edge of the city. The area was sealed off with barbed-wire fences. Through their thorny spaces he made out dense clusters of flamboyants. Emokhai sniffed the air for the hundredth time, trying to ascertain whether it was true that the military governor had acres of richly-kept marijuana farms in the vicinity.

He wound his way to the only pools office in the city where he didn't owe any money. Everyone was talking about the governor's birthday parade. He went into the smoky back room, where a game of poker was solemnly in progress. Marjomi wasn't there. The manager of the pools office said:

'He was in earlier. He had three aces and lost all his money to a flush. I think he's in a bad way.'

Emokhai left the pools office and went to their favourite bar two streets away. When he pushed aside the red and yellow strips of curtain the noise in the bar assaulted him. The place was crowded. All the benches were occupied, there was practically no space to stand, and the air was full of flies. The clamour of voices rose to him. At the bar the manager was having a furious argument with three prostitutes and a truck-pusher. Hi-life music blared from the loudspeakers. Everywhere the clientele were arguing about the governor's real age, about if he had been a good leader, or whether he was merely another thief in office who had not yet been exposed.

Emokhai pushed his way through the sweaty bodies. It was hot in the bar and the ceiling fan only seemed to make the place hotter. He found Marjomi at a far corner, sitting on a high stool, his glass empty, his head jerking feverishly. He seemed quite drunk. He was a thin, fleshless character with veins showing on his neck. As he sat he occasionally launched into a torrent of abuse, accusations and recriminations which were directed both at no one in particular and at every one. Ever since Marjomi's wife ran off with a musclebound truck-pusher he had been out of work. With her departure his luck also seemed to have deserted him. He used to make a varied, if precarious, living gambling at poker and on the pools. He was always generous with his tips: other people more careful, more canny, than he had been had opened up shops on account of his former intuitions. But he was no longer quite the same man. He dabbled now with the prophecies of Nostradamus and the mysticism of Lobsang Rampa. And because of his confusion he had taken to pushing his luck to mad extremes, getting into fights with soldiers, insulting strangers in bars over disagreements about politics, and launching into philosophic disquisitions with women he had never met before. He used to be joyful in his high-spiritedness, but now he was incandescent and disagreeable in his depressions.

Standing behind Marjomi, Emokhai said:

'My friend, I hear you lost all your money.'

Marjomi turned, glared at him, picked up his empty glass, drank from it, and then said:

'I had three aces and lost to a flush.'

'Bad luck.'

'Bad luck to you.'

Emokhai smiled and leaned his heavy frame on the bar. They were silent for a while.

'What happened to you?' Emokhai said at last.

'Nothing.'

'But you were supposed to come to my place.'

'Buy me a drink.'

'I'm broke. We were supposed to go to the hospital.'

'It's too hot to talk business.'

'Are we going or not?'

'After I've had a drink.'

Emokhai stared at him.

'You're mad,' he said, eventually.

Marjomi burst into a cracked sort of laughter.

'It's our governor's birthday. Why are you so serious?'

Emokhai, light-headed with the heat and the sudden invasion of hunger, suppressed his frustration and said:

'I don't know about you, but I'm going.'

'Where?'

'To the hospital.'

Emokhai left the bar, harassed by the flies and the overwhelming smell of stale palm-wine. Outside, the heat surpassed itself. Emokhai couldn't breathe. He crossed the road and waited. He brought out his crumpled packet of filterless cigarettes and lit up. He hated smoking on a hungry stomach. Surrounded by market women and garage touts, by soldiers and military policemen, he thought about Marjomi. He thought about his friend's erratic tempers, his unusually high-grade blood which had virtually saved him from starvation. He thought about money. Marjomi came out of the bar, jerking his head, and then squinted in Emokhai's direction. Emokhai went and stood beneath the shade of a stall, in front of which was a stagnant gutter. He stared at the empty Coke cans and newspaper pages that floated with the algae. Marjomi took his time crossing the road.

'Are you afraid of death?' Emokhai asked him.

At first Marjomi, walking slowly behind Emokhai, didn't say anything. As they went the turbines of the planes roared above them. Emokhai caught a glimpse of a pilot's headgear in the green cockpit.

'Why should I be afraid of death?'

A motorcade with a dozen outriders screamed past them. Luxurious cars followed the motorcade and behind the cars there were armoured tanks.

They passed the High Court, with its bronze statues of the old Empire. They went down roads where ancient statues, symbols of authority, disintegrated beneath the sun and under the onslaught of the sand and wind. They passed an area which used to be a market where slaves were sold a hundred years before. As they went Emokhai felt his nose and lungs getting clogged by the dust and the fumes of the air. He lit another cigarette.

They passed the bank of which it was rumoured that the governor was a major shareholder. Along the Ekenwa Road they passed the chain of supermarkets which the newspapers had said belonged to the governor, but in the name of a non-existent son.

Emokhai shuffled along, staring at the buildings. Behind him Marjomi muttered something about finding attachments. The noise of music from record shops and from the rooms of unemployed bachelors, the panic of the sirens, and the dehydrating heat followed them all the way to the hospital. Emokhai waited under the branches of a barren orange tree, a few yards from the hospital gate, while Marjomi caught up with him. Marjomi, devious, and absent-minded, stumbled down the street with quick movements that didn't seem to get him very far. The expression in his eyes gave him the look of an occasional criminal. He sidled up to Emokhai, rested a hand on his shoulder, and looked over at the Queen Mary Memorial Hospital, with its plaques, its dust-eaten statues, the rusting ambulance vehicles that were broken down in the courtyard, and its flaking signboard. Then he said:

'My friend, there has got to be something wrong with us.'

'What do you mean?'

'Surely there's a better way.'

'What are you grumbling about? You've got expensive blood, man. Let's go.'

And so on that boiling afternoon they went into the hospital. They were treated badly by the nurses, who hustled them into the waiting-room. Emokhai was called

43

first. He shuffled out into one of the crowded blood units. Marjomi sat jerking his head, waving his hands, fretting on the uncomfortable metallic seat. When Emokhai came back in, having sold a pint, he looked very pale. He staggered as he pushed through the waiting-room door. Then he slumped into a chair, shut his eyes, and breathed erratically.

It was a while before they called Marjomi. And before they did he had to make some trouble. He went up to one of the nurses and an argument started.

'I need the money!' he shouted.

'You've sold enough for one week. Do you think we drink it, eh?' the nurse replied, and stormed away.

Marjomi went back into the waiting-room. He began to pace up and down, in a curious frenzy. He was in a bad state that afternoon. He used to be one of the city's tireless workers. When he wasn't at the pools offices, hustling, trying to sell tips, he would be at the garage, rushing people into one taxi or another. He used to get his tips from a very private and arbitrary system of numerology – a system which went to pieces when his wife left him. After that he never sold any more tips: they kept failing. He became known as a bit of a quack. The punters began to joke about how he always sold tips he never bet on himself. At the garage it became just as difficult: because he grew desperate, he overstepped the unwritten rules of touting. The other touts began to regard him as a bit of an irregular fellow. To be a good tout required a special, controlled, passion, a mania for the quick job executed with spontaneous bursts of energy. He had lost his edge. He became listless and damned lazy, given to fits and starts, a man at odds with his own vision of himself.

That was how he looked that afternoon, as he paced up and down, a strange demented energy taking over his movements.

'Why don't you sit still, eh?' Emokhai said. 'You look like a chicken that's lost its head.'

'Mind your own bloody business!' Marjomi replied, sitting down.

After a while a nurse came and called him into the blood unit. He stumbled after her. Indifferently, impatiently, they made him lie on a couch. They jabbed a syringe into a vein in his arm and drew a little amount of blood. Then they wrapped a tight rubber band around his forearm and pumped it up. They made him clench his fist. The nurses were in a hurry. The hospital was jammed with casualties of robberies, encounters with soldiers, victims of glass fights, those afflicted with all manner of diseases, the ill and the dying. All the wards were full up. Patients lay cluttered along the passageways and corridors, moaning and screaming into the red afternoon.

Marjomi began to make flapping gestures with his free arm. He felt very uncomfortable with the tightness of the rubber band.

'Tighten your fist!' the nurse commanded.

He tightened it and they slowly drew his blood up the syringe. Watching made him feel sick; nausea spread from his eyes.

'Keep your eyes open!' the nurse shouted.

He blinked and looked around. He felt he had been dreaming.

'Or you will have a broken needle in your vein!' the nurse added, laughing.

Marjomi kept awake with a great act of will. His blood gathered up the tube and bile rushed to his mouth and he held it there, swaying in the heat of the hospital unit. The flow of his blood up the glass tube always startled him. When they had finished the nurse advised him to eat plenty of protein-giving food.

'Eat fruits as well,' she said, 'or you will become a skeleton with dried skin.'

Marjomi, feeling that he had fallen into a dream rather than woken from one, staggered out of the blood unit, past the waiting-room and out into the street, with the two naira in his hand. Emokhai came after him.

'So you were going, eh?'

Marjomi showed him the two naira he had been paid.

'This is less than what a prostitute gets,' he said, staring vacantly ahead of him.

Then he went out into the noise of roaring planes. When he went under the full glare of the sun he looked dazed. He blinked and staggered, as if he had suddenly gone blind. It was very hot. Even the rusted ambulance vehicles reflected sharp points of light. Marjomi made a strange noise, as if he were recharging himself, then he pushed on into the heat and dust. He kept muttering to himself, stumbling forward, somewhat deranged.

'I feel faint,' he said.

'Take it easy,' replied Emokhai, solid as ever.

'Let's go to a bar. I need a drink.'

'I'm going home.'

'Why?'

'I feel faint too.'

'You're like an ox. How can you faint?'

'What about the parade?'

'What about it?'

'We're supposed to go and try our luck.'

'Let's talk about it later. I feel faint.'

'Let's talk about it now. Are you going or not?'

'Of course I'm going. What can I do with this bloody two naira.'

'So you will be there, eh?'

'Yes. But I need a drink. I don't feel well. I saw the blood flowing up the tube . . .'

'So did I.'

The planes droning overhead increased Emokhai's hunger. Marjomi marched on ahead, tripping on stones.

'We've got to find a job,' Emokhai said.

'There are no jobs in this city.'

'We've got to find an attachment.'

'Where?'

They had just got to the High Court, with its reddening building, when things began to float down from the sky. At first they didn't notice. But when a mass of paper strips fell from the burning sky onto Marjomi's shoulder he gave a strange cry, looked up, and then he collapsed on the roasting dust of the ground. A rich shower of confetti and paper poured down from the planes like a descent of insects in biblical prophecies. Feeling as if he were under an invasion, as if a new war had been declared, Emokhai rushed to his friend who had fainted when the streamers came down.

'What happened to you?' he said, touching Marjomi on the shoulder.

At the moment of contact Marjomi opened his eyes. He had the look of a frightened animal. Then, in a sudden rage, he jumped up. His eyes were liverish. He was in a bad temper. A tortured light glimmered in his eyes. He wobbled and held his head. Looking around with a paranoid gaze, he said:

'I'm going to the bar.'

He staggered down the road without acknowledging his friend's concern, without looking back, and without even removing the red dust that was stamped on the back of his head, on the other side of his face, and all the way down his faded jeans.

Emokhai watched his friend go. Then he stared at the strips of paper that pirouetted towards the ground. He picked up one of the strips. The paper bore a stamped portrait of the governor, a soldier who had reputedly saved the city during a siege in the war. Written under the portrait was the statement: 'We wish you a happy birthday.'

The planes dived, sending shadows everywhere. The cascade of confetti continued. The naked children rushed about trying to pick up as many strips of paper as they could. Emokhai pushed homewards. He passed the formless rubbish dump which seemed to grow bigger every day. He went home under the tireless glare of sunlight, under the shadow of paper strips that fell over the mud huts, that pattered on the heads of all those ghetto-dwellers who hurried, or who slouched, about their business.

2

When he got home Mama Joe told him that Dede had come by earlier.

'Didn't she leave a message?'

'She said she will try again later.'

Emokhai went into his room. He was thirsty. He looked into the green plastic bucket that was beside the cupboard and found that he had no drinking water. From the base to the rim the bucket was glazed with red sediment. The water pipes of the compound had never been repaired since they burst two weeks after their installation three years ago. Emokhai went outside and bought a bucket of water from the owner of the aluminium tank next door. When he came back in he sat on the wooden bed. The stench of the bucket-lavatory wafted in from the backyard. The windows couldn't be opened and the mustiness in the room could almost be tasted. Emokhai breathed in deeply, thinking about money. He stared at the almanac of notable people from his hometown. The almanac was grained over with red dust. While Emokhai thought about money he came to the decision that it was impossible to get rich honestly. Where there is money, there is theft, he said to himself. He got up, went out of the room, fetched some water from the well, and had a bath. He dried himself in the room and got dressed for the parade. He regarded himself in the mirror on the wall. He felt he looked presentable. With his shabby coat on, a cross round his neck, a watch which never worked, and his pair of jeans which were too tight for him, he actually looked like a man trying to hide his desperation.

By the time he got outside he was sweating again. The sun burned relentlessly. Mama Joe, her child tied to her back, was sitting on a low stool. Her wrapper was expertly folded between her legs. She sweated into the large frying pan, in which vegetable oil sizzled, and into which she had been dripping dollops of ground beans for the evening's akara. Her other children, naked and covered in dust, played about the street, with the streamers and strips of paper in chains round their necks.

'Mama Joe,' said Emokhai, 'if Dede should come again tell her to wait for me.

She nodded.

Emokhai left the compound. The sun poured down its rust and fire. The planes free-fell, their metal wingspans green against the ochre sky. Streamers floated above the houses. As he walked under the drone of the circling planes, the thought that it was indeed the governor's birthday had the unexpected effect of cheering him up.

Emokhai became aware of the increased bustle of military vehicles. There were banners over bank fronts congratulating the governor. One of the newspapers had printed, on its front page, an enlarged photograph of the governor as a baby – the baby that would one day save the city.

Articulated lorries ground past. The roads trembled in the grip of careering motorcades and armoured trucks. Jeeps with back-loads of militia blasted the streets with noise.

Over the dry expanse of the square there were crowds

of people. Food-sellers, with basins on their heads, had stopped to watch the parade. The Market Women's Union had turned up in full numbers with placards wishing the governor a happy birthday. Dancers from the interiors of the state, the somersaulters from the creeks which used to be a passageway for the slave trade also turned up with banners. The Agbor dancers, all women, waving blue handkerchiefs over their heads, had also turned up to show their support for the administration. There were bachelor-types, well-dressed, their beards peppered with dust. There was an outer perimeter of tightly bunched soldiers, guns held solidly under their arms, horsewhips dangling from their metallic belts.

The roll and crash of military music obliterated the noises of the city. In front of every statue and monument in the square there stood a soldier. The statues were often of ferocious ancient figures: kings, queens, tyrants, rulers who were slave-traders and who wreaked terror on their people, and who sealed the terror with incredible nets of superstitions and dread rituals.

Emokhai walked against the clamour of drums and brass, studying the crowd, trying to isolate the restless head of Marjomi. Emokhai smiled when he thought of his friend. Marjomi: the gyroscope of heaving crowds, silent as a razor. Marjomi: who can make a living by selling his blood at Queen Mary's Memorial Hospital and by shifting the balances of people's pockets. Marjomi: an unchained agent, who swears that the government had tried to poison him because he was outspoken. Emokhai thought he saw someone like him, someone with one

51

arm shorter than the other, and a head restless like that of a hungry chicken.

Moving slowly past a soldier, smelling the sweat from his starched khaki-green uniform, and the heat from his gun, Emokhai slipped into the crowd and touched Marjomi on the elbow. A total stranger turned a ferocious gaze at Emokhai, who apologized quickly, and ducked back into the crowd. Marjomi: it was just like him to be seen in others without being there himself. Emokhai knew suddenly that Marjomi wouldn't turn up at the parade.

The military drill began. Three lines of soldiers, fully decked, their ranks neat in regularity, stamped themselves into clouds of red dust. They stamped with robotic uniformity, right- and left-turning, their boots covered with dust, their guns gleaming under the fierce sun. An officer, staff under armpit, inspected them. The soldiers had sweated, had dried out, had sweated again, and the endless process of it had left a quality of hungry brutality on their faces. The planes droned above. School children, herded out in great numbers, sweltered under the harsh sunlight. Gun salutes blasted the air.

Emokhai edged his way through the temper of the crowd till he got to a group of people who were the only ones fearless or stupid enough to talk while the national anthem was being sung. A thick-set man wearing a white safari-suit and sandals seemed to be the centre of the group. He spoke with windmill movements of his arms, jabbing the air, accidentally knocking off people's hats and muttering apologies, while froth gathered at the edges of his mouth. Emokhai pushed closer. The drums trembled the ground and the seismic brass rattled his teeth.

'What does he think he is doing, eh?' the frothing man said loudly.

A few terracotta heads turned in the man's direction. Red eyes regarded him and, in the space of a gaze, travelling from his cheap sandals to his dust-coloured hair, they took in all they needed to know, and dismissed him.

The frothing man continued:

'Just because he is a military governor does every birthday have to be a big parade? Stamping dust over the city. Grinding their monster vehicles up and down the bad roads. How old is he that the city has to come to a halt!'

The circle around the man widened. He had become, in an instant, a mad man, and therefore interesting. The trumpets blasted. A shower of lights flashed from the stand. The governor climbed onto the wooden band-stand and the sweating crowd cheered. Soldiers solidified their guard round the plinth. The frothing man was relentless.

'Look at him. Pompous blighter! Fat like an ox! Full of the people's food. And to think that he robbed one of our banks during the war. We are mad. All of us that condone this nonsense are mad!' he shouted, his voice rising with a rough energy.

Every time he raised his arms a jagged circle of sweat showed beneath his armpits.

I wish I had blood as rare as Marjomi's, thought Emokhai as he inched towards the man. Pushing aside the vision of the crowd setting upon him, Emokhai was about to touch the man when he burst into another crescendo of insults. The band, stepping up after the governor gave a salute of terrible authority, brought forth a thunderous roll of military music. The metal boots crashed on the ground with multiplied energies. The precision was marvellous to behold. In the middle of the grounds, where the nation's flag fluttered, engrained with a progressive rust, the children waved listlessly. They waved little red flags on sharpened pegs. They waved without purpose and without any relation to the crashing music.

An officer bellowed a command. The trumpets sounded. The governor came forward to the microphone. The trumpets sounded again. The governor raised his arm, commanding his trumpeters to cease. Then with another wave he ordered the crowd to be silent. He wanted to be heard. The fact that he was once a boxer was manifest in his stance.

The man in the safari-suit sucked his teeth. Emokhai knew he had to move fast. The military governor, who from afar looked a bit like a warthog, proceeded to speak. He spoke with great emphasis, slowly, and yet no one could make out what he was saying. The children waved their flags. The governor made a curt gesture with his hands. His face glistened. The planes, which had been specks in the sky, came roaring past. Spangles of paper strips sailed down on the bandstand, over the governor's head, and all over the parade grounds. The governor fulminated at the error and barked orders which were misunderstood. The band struck up. If the governor's stance was that of a boxer, then his opponent was the chaos he had created in order to rule.

The children waved.

Emokhai touched the man in the safari-suit. The touch was sufficient. Then he carefully pushed his way through the crowd, while keeping an eye on the man. He was at a safe distance when the man discovered his loss, and erupted. He ran this way and that. Then he began, frantically, to search the ground.

When the crowd descended on the man Emokhai understood why the children waved their flags with such disconnected regularity. And when the man emerged, his suit in tatters, he was as defiant as ever. He cursed with such vehemence that the children stopped waving and stared at him. He swore at the thief, he cursed the damned city, and he poured abuse on all the people who had laid hands on him.

The planes swooped past low and drowned out his curses. The governor, on the bandstand, was receiving honours, medallions, and gifts from the powerful people of the state. His neck was weighed down with yellow ribbons and medals from the Department of Finance, citations from state universities, all set up and censored under his personal supervision. He received gold necklaces from secret societies and multinational concerns. The music rolled. When the hour of gifts passed he went and unveiled a bronze statue of himself, which would stand besides all the others that were fading under the heat of the sun.

The planes came again. The children ducked. Emokhai ducked with them. And when they looked up they saw that rags were falling from the planes, like glutinous flakes from the sky. The governor launched into a brisk speech, while the schoolchildren – every one of them with their different sores – were entirely bewildered. The band played a rolling processional beat and marched their way round the field to the gate. The governor walked delicately down the steps from the bandstand towards his limousine. The car, green, bulletproofed, with tinted windows, automatic telephones, a fridge, and a set of decanters, was arrowed like an instrument of precise comforts. An aide opened the back door. The governor saluted his officers, stamped, and ducked into the vehicle. The celebrations had just begun. The other state officials got into their vehicles. The outriders started their sirens. The motorcade moved slowly out of the grounds. The governor's limousine was in the middle of the convoy. And when his car drove past the people couldn't see him. They could not see what it was he transformed into, what secret physical corruptions crept over his features, or what his monstrosities were.

The children waved.

It was so hot that they had stopped sweating. They waved their flags as if, wholly without conviction, they were trying to attract the governor's attention. And afterwards, as they dispersed over the field, each to their different hungry homes, they carried the rags and paper strips with them as mementoes of the year when the governor turned fifty.

Emokhai left the parade grounds with the children. As he went down the streets he felt vaguely bitter, he felt the temptation to hit something. There were dust-clouds everywhere. When he emerged from the dust he felt whittled, he felt he reappeared a shade more invisible.

On his way back home he bumped into Marjomi outside a betting shop. He was drunk, feverish, and he had a tortured look on his face. He kept jerking his head in unison with his arm. He had a thin woman with him whom Emokhai had never seen before.

'What happened to you?' Emokhai asked.

'Mind your own business.'

'But I waited for you at the parade.'

'I was busy.'

'Doing what?'

'Losing money,' the thin woman said before Marjomi could speak.

'Shut up, you hear?' Marjomi said to the woman.

Emokhai studied her. She was not attractive. She had a bony face and hollow eyes. She wore a tight blue dress which emphasized her boniness. She had a bad-tempered expression on her face which curiously matched Marjomi's restlessness.

'So you were gambling when I was waiting for you, eh?'

Marjomi tossed his head.

'This time I lost to four aces.'

'All the money?'

'Not all.'

'All,' the woman said.

'Shut up!'

The woman walked on ahead and stopped. She regarded both of them. Then she turned her head away in a gesture of contempt.

'I still feel faint,' Marjomi said, when the woman was out of hearing range.

'Go home and get some rest.'

'I can't.'

'Why not?'

'Because I am sure something is going to happen.'

'What?'

'I don't know. Something good.'

'What about if you faint?'

'Then I will get up.'

'You're going crazy, you know.'

'I know.'

'You are a bastard for not coming to the parade.'

'What did I miss?'

Emokhai showed him the wallet he had stolen. Marjomi reached for it, but Emokhai withdrew his hand.

'We could have had a good day.'

Marjomi shrugged.

'I need to get a job,' he said, 'I need to fly under a flag.'

'What job, what flag?'

'A flag of power.'

Emokhai put the wallet back into his pocket.

'You're not serious,' he said, and began to leave.

Marjomi caught his arm and, looking earnestly at him with fevered eyes, said:

'The nurse said I must eat well.'

'Then eat well.'

'I'm going to the hospital tomorrow.'

Emokhai looked at the pale, almost fleshless face of his friend. Then a little angrily he said:

'So?'

'How can I eat well when I don't have a job?'

Emokhai felt he had to control his temper.

'What has that got to do with me?'

Marjomi released Emokhai from his curiously obsessive grip. Jerking his head, changing his stance, he said:

'Borrow me two naira.'

Emokhai began to laugh. He was exasperated, he was furious, and he felt like hitting Marjomi, but instead he laughed. Marjomi stared at him impassively, almost as if he were daring Emokhai to be mean, to be violent.

Mechanically, almost unaware of what he was doing, Emokhai brought out the stolen wallet and gave Marjomi two naira. Marjomi pocketed the money, slapped his friend on the shoulder, and said:

'Let's go and have a drink.'

Emokhai, at that moment, felt as if he had been suddenly released from a spell. The harshness of the lights hurt his eyes. He felt confused.

'I'm going home,' he said, not moving. 'But I will see you later.'

Marjomi nodded and staggered off towards the woman, who had been waiting impatiently near a kiosk. When Emokhai turned to see how they looked together, they were gone.

When he got near his street he found the area full of soldiers. They were jumping off the backs of military lorries. They rampaged the seedy brothels that were two storeys high, and that looked as if all the weight of such cheap fornication would topple them. Most of the soldiers were drunk and rowdy on account of the governor's birthday. Emokhai passed a private who was dragging a woman with him. The woman, her neck rigid, laughed hysterically.

Emokhai went into his room and emptied the contents of the wallet on the bed. He was sorely disappointed with what he found. The wallet contained several business cards, three naira, and plenty of copper coins. Emokhai swore. Then he began to laugh. He should have known better. He should have known that those who talk too much, who are too loud, too eager to criticize, tend to have nothing. Emokhai took the wretched wallet out into the backyard and threw it over the wall, behind which was a festering pile of garbage. He went back into the house and locked his door. As he went past his neighbour's room he glimpsed the governor's face on the small television set. Emokhai stopped. The governor was talking about his victories during the war. His bulging face glistened with sweat.

Emokhai, standing outside the neighbour's room, his face pressed to the grilled window, watched television for a while. Then he became aware of curious sounds coming from the dry-cleaner's room, two doors down. The dry-cleaner, a Rosicrucian, chanted vowel sounds. Outside, the ochre dust stiffened the clothes drying on the lines. Emokhai went to the housefront and watched the planes. Mama Joe had gone to the market for the early evening shopping. Her stall was empty. Waiting for Dede, fighting the dust, he became aware of his hunger. He listened to the soothing vowel sounds from the dry-cleaner's room. He decided to go and get something to eat.

As he left the compound for the nearest bukka, it struck him that all natural life – the cockroaches, the cats, the dogs, the leaves of the stunted orange tree – was being buried in dust. He found a bukka, he ate silently and, feeling better, he left. Outside, the lights hit him. And with eyes that had been focused on the food in the dark bukka, he saw the city as if for the first time. He saw the red dust and, on the zinc rooftops, he saw patterns of an empire stifled in history.

Thinking about the football teams he might bet on, he headed for his favourite bar where he hoped to have a drink with Marjomi. He was about to enter the bar when a woman's voice called him from across the road. He turned and feeling instantly lighter he realized that it was Dede.

'Where have you been?' he asked, as if he had seen her only ten minutes ago.

'Looking for you,' she said, crossing the road.

She had once been Marjomi's girlfriend and had passed into Emokhai's hands. He had grown tired of her rather rapidly. They went out for a month. Her habits were more expensive than Emokhai thought she was worth. She used to spend most of her time reading American magazines. She was also sexually so insatiable that when they were alone he couldn't do anything else. He couldn't get enough work done. His system of numerology, derived from Marjomi's, began to crash in digits of sevens. He lost his job. She, on the other hand, refusing to do any work of any kind, drifted around the squalid compound in her moth-eaten evening gown. Then one day, during an argument, he discovered that she was a potential murderer. She had picked up a knife and thrown it so hard that if it weren't for the nitrogen of fear mixed with luck he would have been pinned to the cabinet, his heart divided. When she left his life she first made sure she wrecked his room. They didn't speak to one another for two years. Then recently they picked up an old thread of friendship and became amicable towards one another. He owed her fifty naira.

As she crossed the road Emokhai watched her. She wore a single wrapper and cheap lace blouse. Her earrings were bulbous and her lips were smeared red. What was left of her beauty was buried in fat. She had rings of flesh round her neck. Her eyes had almost become the colour of the city's dust. She had a permanent expression of sarcasm on her face. She moved with a calculated sway of her generous hips.

'Emokhai, how now?'

'I'm fine.'

He eyed her. When she came over he put his arm around her waist, but she pushed him away.

'I'm going to have a drink,' he said.

She stood outside the bar, hesitant. Emokhai went in, swishing his way past the striped curtains. The smell of spilt palm-wine made him thirsty. Without looking to see if Dede had come in with him, he pushed his way to the bar and ordered two beers.

'I'm not drinking beer,' she said from behind him.

'What then?'

'Stout.'

He changed the order. When the drinks arrived they began to look for a vacant table. The place was packed as ever. People with drinks in one hand, a cigarette in the other, stood against the walls. The lights were dull. The ceiling fan rotated slowly, barely stirring the dust on its blades. Voices rose from everywhere in rough waves. In one corner several men competed for a prostitute's attention. In another corner several prostitutes competed for the attentions of two businessmen. People laughed violently. Raucous jokes surfaced amongst the voices. Emokhai pushed forwards through the crowd, spilling his drink on people's shoes and trousers. No one noticed. When Emokhai got to a far corner of the bar, where there was space to stand, he saw the thin woman that had been with Marjomi. She stood against the bar. She wore green earrings and her lips were purple. She wore a red dress, tight around the hips and awkward at the back. She was talking rather furiously, as if at the barman, and her gestures, accentuated by her long red fingernails, were jagged like those of a wild cat.

Emokhai had almost reached her when he realized that, of all people, Marjomi was sitting on a high stool, his shirt torn, his neck plastered, his head on his hands, his hands on the bar. He looked like a man unsuccessfully trying to escape from a barrage of criticism.

'So why did you go and fight, eh?'

'Leave me alone.'

'Why you fight three people, eh?'

'Shut up.'

'You want to die? Are you tired of living? What about your mother?'

'Go away.'

'Where did you get money from?'

'Where do you think?'

'You went to the hospital again?'

'Eat shit.'

'At this rate it's only piss that will be floating in your body.'

'So what?'

'Why don't you get a job?'

'From where?'

'Be a labourer.'

'I don't have the strength.'

Emokhai touched Marjomi on the shoulder and said: 'You are too lazy.'

Marjomi looked up and his face brightened.

'Emokhai!' he said, as if he were seeing his friend for the first time in years. 'Where have you been?'

'What do you mean? I've been here.'

'Here?'

'No. Around.'

'My friend, buy me a drink. This woman is giving me too much trouble.'

'Who is giving you trouble?' the thin woman said. Then turning to Emokhai: 'He went to the hospital today. Again.'

'I know.'

'How?'

'I went with him.'

She looked at both men. Dede pushed her way into their midst.

'Marjomi, how now?' she said tentatively.

Marjomi stared at her a long time, silently. There was a bewildered look on his face. Emokhai ordered another drink. When the drink arrived he gave it to Marjomi, then turned to Dede and said:

'Come to my place later.'

'What for?'

'So I can pay you back the money I owe.'

'Pay me now.'

'It's at home.'

She eyed him knowingly.

'Will you come?'

She nodded. Emokhai smiled. During all this the thin woman had been haranguing Marjomi. She criticized him for getting into a fight, complained about his fleshlessness, about his dirty clothing, his uncombed hair, his patchy complexion, his excessive drinking. Marjomi sat hunched, a tortured expression on his face, his head jerking involuntarily. His lips quivered. He drank steadily. When he finished his beer he ordered another one and asked the thin woman to pay. She refused. The drink was served. The barman asked for the money. Marjomi stared at the girl.

'You want me to go to hospital again?'

'Do what you want,' she said, sucking her teeth.

'So you won't pay?'

'No. I'm not your slave.'

'What about you, Emokhai? Will you pay for me?'

'I have no money, my friend.'

Marjomi glared at him. They all stayed silent.

'I will pay,' Dede said, quietly.

Marjomi didn't take his eyes off Emokhai.

'I don't want your money,' he said.

'Why not?' asked Dede.

'Because I don't.'

'Isn't my money good enough for you anymore?'

'Why don't you go and give it to your truck-pusher?'

'What truck-pusher?'

'You are confusing her with your wife,' Emokhai said.

'She is just like her, full of bad luck,' Marjomi said, spitting.

Then, for no apparent reason, he began to insult Dede. He said she was too fat, that she was just the type of woman who preferred truck-pushers and soldiers. He went on talking himself into a feverish state, his eyes bleary, his mood cantankerous, while the barman bugged him about the money for the drink. Marjomi went on and on, cursing, swearing at the governor, insulting the thin woman, whom he said reminded him of one of the more vicious nurses at the blood unit. It was when he took to shouting at strangers, complaining about the sourness of their faces, that people began to take an unhealthy interest in their group.

'Tell your friend to shut up,' one of the drunken clientele said, 'or we will ground him into the dust.'

Marjomi was encouraged. He shouted on, jerking his bad elbow in their faces, till Dede, unable to bear it anymore, slammed some money on the counter, and told Marjomi to be quiet.

'You're getting fat,' he said, 'like a tyre.'

Dede stared at him, put the change in her purse, and then slapped Marjomi on the face. He grabbed her and was about to hit her when Emokhai caught his hand. A cross-eyed man thrust himself forward.

'You touch her and you die,' he threatened, and returned to his drinking circle.

Dede finished her drink and began to leave. Emokhai urged her to stay, but she was past listening. She pushed her way through the crowd. One of the men with the cross-eyed fellow made a grab for her breasts. Emokhai drew up to the man. A fight seemed imminent. But with Dede disappearing out of the bar more urgent concerns called him. He hurried out and caught up with her just as she was about to enter a taxi.

'Come to my place later. Please, eh.'

She got in and slammed the door. The taxi drove off. She didn't look back.

When Emokhai got back into the bar he found commotion. A crowd surrounded the far corner. And from the midst of the wall of bodies came Marjomi's shrill and demented voice. Emokhai pushed his way over. Apparently Marjomi had been pouring out a torrent of blasphemies and innuendoes, calling the military governor a thief and all the citizens of the state cowards. Many voices rose against him, threatening him. The thin woman stood by, watching helplessly.

'I don't care if all of you belong to the secret societies of cowards!' Marjomi shouted. 'The worst you can do is kill me!'

'We will kill you, if you're not careful,' someone said.

'Note his face,' Marjomi said.

'Take it easy, Marjomi.'

'Leave me alone, Emokhai,' screamed Marjomi. 'I hate that woman of yours.' And then, as if there had been no interruption, he shouted: 'All you cowards, members of pox-ridden fraternities, ghouls and ghosts, corrupt citizens, selfish and greedy, morons, pimps, slave-traders, arse-lickers!'

It got worse. The barman became quite bad-tempered. His indulgence had been worn thin.

'Just because of one drink!' Marjomi roared. 'And all my friends, my woman, every one, deserts me!'

Emokhai ordered a beer, hoping it would quieten down his friend. But Marjomi was beyond quieting. His neck taut, he shouted:

'Does anybody want blood!'

'Shut up,' people said.

'If anybody wants blood I'll sell a pint for one naira!'

'Save your cheap blood,' someone said.

'MY BLOOD IS NOT CHEAP!' Marjomi yelled.

The barman increased the volume of the music, drowning out Marjomi's weird voice. His mouth moved, his eyes widened, the veins of his neck stuck out, and no one heard what he said. Emokhai tried to calm him down, but Marjomi pushed him away and sent him crashing into the gathered crowd. The people grew angry. They pressed towards Marjomi, who seemed to relish the idea of being beaten, and Emokhai needed all his might, all his tact, to hold them back. Marjomi, in the meantime, became increasingly possessed. He kept uttering a curious, frightening, high-pitched scream, as if he were trying to wake up from a heated nightmare, a terrible hallucination. He seemed quite mad.

'Take my blood!' he kept saying, over and over again.

It got so bad, what with his jerking and fretting on the

high stool, that he fell over, knocked his head on the edge of the bar, and began to kick and fight on the floor, as if the whole world were out to get him. It took five people to hold him down. When he had been completely pinned down, the barman came over to him and said:

'If you don't shut up, you madman, we will throw you out. And you can stay out. I like you, but you're going too far.'

With sweat pouring into his eyes, with him blinking as if he were fighting unconsciousness, and with the voice of a frightened, submissive child, he said:

'I'm fine now.'

They let him go. He got up, dusted himself, and drank quietly. The thin woman regarded him with brightened eyes. He did not speak. He was not spoken to. Emokhai tapped him on the shoulder and hurried out in anticipation of Dede's possible visit.

3

When he got home he cleaned out his room. He dressed the bed. He separated his washed clothes from his filthy ones. He listened to some music on his transistor radio while counting the small change he often threw into a black boot. He played around with his system of numerology and came up with some arbitrary forecasts for the following week's football bets. He was listening to the combined sounds of the music and the vowel chantings of the Rosicrucian next door, when he heard someone knocking.

'Come in!' he said.

Dede swept into the room, smiling.

'So what happened to your stupid friend?'

'Don't mind him. Poverty is driving him mad.'

'He is a goat. He's too proud. So what if a soldier used to be my boyfriend?'

'Forget him.'

She sat down on the only chair in the room.

'Why you never come visit me?' she asked.

'Things hard. Money scarce.'

'What about the money you owe me?'

'I will pay you.'

'When?'

'Soon.'

'I hear that you went to the hospital again.'

'Forget the hospital.'

'All that blood.'

'Forget the blood.'

She fell silent. He looked her over. He noticed that she sat with her legs pointed sideways.

'You still read all those useless magazines?'

'None of your business.'

He went over and sat on her knees. She smelt good. Her face was fleshy, her breasts proud, her hair perfumed. But he also noticed the wrinkles fashioned on her face by all the hardships, the dry winds, and the red dust. The last thing he had heard about her wasn't that she used to go out with a soldier, but that she had been with five of them. They said she made a lot of money out of it and that she was going into business. They also said that when she went home after the session she walked as if she had crabs between her legs. The men began to avoid her. She began to put on too much weight.

70

But he was hungry and as he touched her face he realized, with a shock, that he hadn't been with a woman for a long time.

'Won't you offer me something to drink?'

'What do you want?'

'Stout,' she said.

He took two empty bottles and went next door to the shop where they sold alcohol and kerosene. When he got back she was sitting on the bed. The room was hot. The planes droned above the rusted zinc rooftops.

He opened the drinks, poured hers into a glass and gave it to her, brushing her thighs with his elbow. He drank from the bottle. She emptied her glass in one gulp and then stretched out on the bed.

He got up and locked the door. She did not look desirable. She was fat around the arms. Her thighs looked too solid. Her neck was lined with rings of flesh. While he studied her he smelt the room as if he were a stranger to it. The red dust lurked in the air, had permeated the clothes, the lightbulb, and had engrained the walls. She did not look desirable but he willed desire. He imagined her naked, imagined his arousal, and felt himself moving into her warm and moist interiors. He went towards her, smiling, asking how she was, saying everything but what he had tricked himself into wanting the most. It wasn't till she knocked his hands away from beneath her wrapper, and locked her fingers around his throat, that he realized just how hungry he was.

'What's the matter' he asked, prising her fingers from round his neck, and urging his hand up her wrapper, moving gently up her legs.

71

She kneed him in the ribs and for a moment he saw the white flash of her underclothes. The knee hurt him and he was about to lash out at her when he noticed the curiously vacant expression on her face, as if she were completely oblivious of what he might do to her.

So he tried the gentle approach. He asked about her mother, her job (she had been made redundant; he knew this), and about her life in general. She remained distant. He felt his way up her again, holding his breath, as if his breathing might, for some reason, make her change her mind. He fingered aside her underclothes and played around the lips of her interiors. She was not moist. Unaccountably, he became aware of the planes droning overhead. They seemed to be flying lower and lower. When it finally occurred to him that she was dry he stopped.

'What's wrong?' he asked.

He was afraid. He was scared that she was completely beyond being aroused by him. He tried again. She lay still, impassive. She gave him a sidelong look and then she got up.

'So you won't give me the money?'

'Tomorrow.'

'Your tomorrow never ends.'

'Tomorrow.'

'I'm going to see my sister.'

She picked up her things. He tried to stop her. He held her from behind, kissing her fleshy neck, and tried to get her back on the bed. He eventually did. He struggled over her and tried to pin her down. Then he tried to loosen his trousers and tear off her wrapper. She kept rocking him, throwing him off-balance. He struggled and sweat dripped from him onto her bared breasts. His sweat was red and it occurred to him that he was sweating blood. Suddenly, making a powerful noise, and with surprising energy, she tossed him off her. Then she got up, opened the door wide, and stood in the middle of the room, her hands on her hips. He collapsed in frustration and watched her.

'I'm going!' she announced.

He got out of bed. She went out of the room, clicking her heels. He followed her up the street, past the brothel, the mechanic's shed, the garbage heaps, and they said nothing to one another as they went. The planes flew in the air, circling the city. The adults and the children were bored with their interminable displays.

'How long are they going to celebrate the thief's birthday?' she said, bitterly.

'Why do you give me so much trouble, eh?'

She looked at him as if he were a complete stranger. A plane, flying low, cast a swift shadow over her. She looked up, then looked at him again. Her lips were curled, pressed tight, as if speech were an act performed under duress.

'Didn't you hear what the soldiers did to me?'

Emokhai was confused.

'What did they do to you?'

'Didn't you hear? Everyone heard.'

Her emphasis changed the slant of what he had heard. Bewildered, he said:

'I heard.'

'Do you think I am made of wood?'

He said nothing. He was scared. He wanted to go back. He suddenly didn't want to be seen with her. She looked at him without warmth and in her eyes he saw little networks of red and green blood-vessels.

'I'll be seeing you,' she said.

And as she turned he noticed a plane free-falling in the air. The engine had been stalled and as the plane somersaulted no one noticed that its engine had, for once, failed. He watched the plane as it fell, mesmerized by the daring joke of it all. Then the engine started, the plane swooped and described an arc. Emokhai turned to reply to Dede and when he saw, out of the corner of his eyes, the plane crash on the thatch houses of the ghetto, he didn't comprehend what he had witnessed. He heard the momentous crash in retrospect. Dede walked on, oblivious to the thunderous sounds of metal on col- lapsing houses. Then a massive cloud of red dust, plaster and smoke obscured her as she disappeared round a corner. When Emokhai looked he saw the rear of the plane jutting out from the top of devastated huts and bungalows. In the sky the other planes flew softly in formation, like birds in August, like cattle egrets at the beginning of harmattan.

4

Later in the evening troops of soldiers came and woke up the inhabitants of the street. They had come to remove the plane and bury their companion. The soldiers had a special mania that evening. They rounded up the people of the street, roughening them up where necessary. The inhabitants stood with their children and their motley property around them, refugees in their own city. It was a while before the fire-service arrived. The lights were cut in the area. The soldiers went about the business of evacuation as if the street were a war-zone. Mama Joe, unable to find her son, wailed up and down the place.

On television the governor, looking both serene and pensive, flanked on one side by the Chief Justice of the state, and on the other side by a bishop, unveiled another statue of himself before a large crowd near Queen Mary's Memorial Hospital. The statue, made of bronze-ore and smelted in Rome, did not look like the governor at all. After the unveiling, the crowd burst into cheering. It was rumoured that he came to the street to see the plane accident. And if no one saw him, if he couldn't do anything about the unfortunate incident, it was because of his chief opponent, the chaos which he had created in order to rule. The plane stayed stuck all night. And because of the evacuation, because of the mood of the soldiers, Emokhai decided to find somewhere else to sleep.

That night, leaving his property behind like one who insists on starting anew, and with no dreams of succeeding, he sought the woman through the city. He sought her in the bars and brothels where they said she could be found drinking, her protuberant stomach rocking in forced laughter. He didn't find her. He decided to seek Marjomi. At the bar the wife of the manager, a wizened woman, told him what had happened.

She told him about Dede, and how on her way home

soldiers had descended on her. When she saw them coming at her she cut herself in the neck with a razor. The story had reached them in the bar and Marjomi, feverish and tormented, had screamed that they should take blood from him. They were in the same blood group. They had put Marjomi in a taxi and had him rushed to the hospital. It was his second time that day.

Emokhai set off immediately. When he got to the hospital he was met by an oversexed-looking nurse, who seemed bored by everything under the sun, and who wouldn't allow him in to see Dede and Marjomi. He sat in the waiting room for what seemed like days. He slept, woke up, and decided to go for a walk. He went up the illustrious streets, where expensive hotels overlooked vast lawns, and where fields of African roses hid the luxuriant golf courses. He made his way to the forest and went to the watch-shed in the area where the governor was believed to have his well-kept marijuana farms. The watch-night was a one-eyed fellow with a weather-beaten face. He eyed Emokhai curiously and said:

'What do you want?'

'I want to buy some herbs.'

'What herbs?'

'The ones that give good dreams in broad daylight.'

The watch-night smiled.

'As you see me,' he said, 'I have two degrees. I am the most over-qualified watchman in the world. But do I grumble?'

'No,' Emokhai said.

'I sit here from morning till night, dreaming I watch

over these farms. I close my eyes to all the things that are
going on. But do I complain?'

'No.'

'Have you come here before?'

'No.'

'Sit down then.'

Emokhai sat on a stool. The old man, his one eye wise
and serene, began to talk. He talked for no particular
reason. He talked as if Emokhai were an old friend who
had just stepped in from the night. The old man talked
about the governor's poultry farm, about the hotel where
the most dazzling collection of cars brought invisible
guests to parties which rocked the city every night. He
talked about those who had been shot, about the
unmarked graves of the state's vanished enemies, and
about the farms created and protected by the governor's
money. He said:

'My son, we are living in wicked times. I have lived out
my life. Now I just dream.'

He was silent for a while.

'What was it you wanted?'

'Some herbs.'

'Oh yes.'

He reached for a bundle in a corner of the shed. He
measured a quantity of leaves. He said:

'If you're caught it's life imprisonment, you know.'

'I know.'

Emokhai took the leaves wrapped in a piece of
newspaper, paid the old man, and left.

When he got back to the hospital there was another

nurse on duty. She said he could see Dede on the condition that he didn't wake her. Dede was in bed, still in a coma, surrounded by tubes. He watched her breathing gently and he wept. Marjomi was nowhere around. The nurse said he had gone. Emokhai stayed watching over Dede till the nurses asked him to leave. He didn't want to leave so they had to get the watch-nights to come and throw him out.

An hour later Emokhai left the hospital. He had no idea where he was going to spend the night. He roamed the darkening city, his stomach grumbling. He wandered down streets littered with celebrations of the governor's birthday. He went from bar to bar looking for Marjomi. Eventually he went to Marjomi's room in the ghetto, in the depths of the city. When he got there he found the door wide open. Marjomi was asleep on the bed, with his shoes still on. Emokhai shut the door, lit a candle, and watched over his sleeping friend. Emokhai marvelled at the gentle ferocity of his spirit. Marjomi slept deeply, his lips pursed, his face completely devoid of its tortured expressions. He slept like one for whom sleep was invented.

Emokhai waited patiently for his friend to wake up. He leafed through the confusion of books scattered about the room. There were books on magic, alchemy, letter-writing, books on fortune-telling, on how to communicate with spirits, a complete guide to palmistry, and the sixteen lessons of a correspondence course called *Turning Experience Into Gold*.

Marjomi woke up suddenly. He saw Emokhai sitting solidly on the chair and he smiled. They ate beans and garri soaked in water, without exchanging a word. When they finished Marjomi lit a mosquito coil and they went to the housefront with his transistor radio. Listening to music, Emokhai rolled up, while Marjomi watched the sky. They smoked the marijuana from the governor's secret farms quietly into the night of the red city.

Stars of the New Curfew

I AM NOT sure when my nightmares began. Sometimes I feel certain that it wasn't when I left the town of W., where I attended secondary school. There were no jobs available then for people of my qualification and as my parents had died during the war I had no one to sponsor my further education. So I did a correspondence course in salesmanship and joined an insurance firm. It folded two months after I began working with them. With no options open to me I had no choice but to earn my living by selling rather dubious locally made medicines at various markets and on the molue buses that career all over Lagos.

At first I did not like the job. The money was insecure. I did not believe in the medicines and most certainly did not use them myself. I felt it was wrong of me to persuade people to buy them. But when I got thrown out of the room I rented, and after I had spent six weeks sleeping under the infamous Iddo Bridge with goats and reticent goatherds, I began to change my mind. No one bothered that I suffered and starved. Why should anyone complain if they were stupid enough to buy the medicines I sold them? Do not believe it when they say that suffering improves you. To some extent it might do. But beyond that it sobers you, hardens you.

The Nightmare of Salesmen

I began to sell medicines with a special vengeance. I devised all kinds of methods for attracting people's attention. I dressed like a clown. I set off fireworks. I developed the most sensational dances and songs to accompany my sales talks. I spent all my energy thinking up new tricks. I practised always. I became so obsessed that I would, in my spare time, take to selling people anything – from empty matchboxes to burnt-out candles. The credulity of people amazed me. I seemed to have stumbled upon a limitless area of possibilities. The prelude to my talks became so fantastic that crowds gathered around me whenever I performed. People would stop on their way to work, market-women with impossible loads on their heads would pause for several minutes; children late for school would be later still in the time they spent watching me.

Sometimes I think I missed my real vocation, but I am not wholly sure what it could have been. Maybe in another society, in a different time, I might have been well regarded as an actor. It's hard to tell. Anyway, my performances became so successful that people would stop and watch me, but they didn't buy very much of the medicine I was supposed to be selling. It was rather odd. My comrades in sales, whom I thought were jealous of my success, used to tease me by saying that I was an actor, an artist, but not a salesman. For a long time I missed the real point of their distinction. It was only when I was threatened with the sack for selling so few medicines that I began to realize that there was something wrong with my methods.

My other comrades, for example, put a third as much effort into their performances but sold three times as many medicines. It was a bit of a mystery. One of them, whom I suspected of being the most jealous of the lot, and whom I also suspected instigated the threat of sacking me, would begin his talk by speaking in an odd nasal accent. He sounded like the voices of masquerades. Sometimes he would hold a flag up in the air, wave it, and would proceed with simple jokes about the flag, would get passers-by laughing, and before their laughter got too far he would switch to a hard selling of the medicines. It always worked. Another comrade, I discovered, used the dreadful device of having lots of friends amongst the passers-by who would come up and, praising the medicines, purchase slightly unreasonable quantities. People always took it as a good sign and this counted more in terms of persuasion than all my circus tricks put together.

A hungry man never does things by halves. I made sure I got better acquainted with my colleagues. I flattered them endlessly. I learned their surprisingly simple methods and soon began to execute them myself.

But I didn't execute them with moderation. I overdid them. I strained at them. I got too many acquaintances, whom I had to pay, to be amongst the passers-by. Then I began to combine my old tricks with the new ones. I became known as a salesman. Whenever I started my acts, people soon began to complete my opening lines. For a while I did well. I moved into better accommodation – two rooms in the ghetto. I bought myself good clothes. I began to contemplate opening my own business, manufacturing my own medicines at home, and keeping the profits for myself. I made plans. Slowly I put them into action. I worked harder. But it was only after some time had passed, when people were beginning to get used to my methods, when some of my accomplices had been unmasked and beaten by duped market-women, that I started to realize I was becoming a victim of my real success. The worst thing that happened was not that some of my accomplices, who were meant to mingle with the crowds and be as ordinary as possible, turned out to be pickpockets who capitalized on my ability to draw people. That was bad enough, because after they had been caught and flogged they lied that they were working for me. People immediately assumed that I was the chief pickpocket, the main organizer. This, however, didn't happen too often, because I got rid of the bad accomplices. But for a time when I appeared the people who remembered screamed abuse at me and sometimes chased me from that section of the market. Mercifully, there are plenty of people in the world and human beings are notorious for having such a short memory.

This meant that I had to keep changing the dubious companies I worked for. During that time I sold medicines for children's diseases, I sold ointment, malaria tablets, phials for yellow fever and dysentery, and books. I kept my methods. It was when I moved into the business of selling ringworm medicines that my real troubles began. Firstly, it shocked me how many people suffered from ringworm, threadworm, rashes, and eczema. The sufferers were all poor. What stunned me however was that I had been selling fake ringworm medicines which actually multiplied ringworm. A woman came to me screaming one day at the market while I was in the second stage of my sales talk. She bared her back and said she had only two rashes of ringworm before and now she was covered in them. Her face was a lacework, a net, a concentric rash of ringworm. I kept trying to get away from her. She frightened me. She looked misbegotten and deformed.

Three days later other people, faces veiled with hats, came to me and cursed me for the rashes that had broken out over their bodies. It was quite scary seeing a horde of worm-eaten people pouring at me every day at work. It got so bad that when people came forward to buy the medicines I often thought they were about to attack me. Then one day an awful thing happened. I had been selling my medicines rather successfully in the market when a woman brought her three children to me. The woman wore a yellow head-tie over a tattered wig. The children looked so wretched, with their swollen stomachs that it was clear they had little to eat, and what they did eat was devoid of nourishment. The money that could have been spent on feeding them a little better had been used to buy medicines. The children were covered in welts so big and red, so obscene, that I couldn't possibly believe it was ringworm. It seemed more like ring*snake*. I think I screamed when I saw the magnified welts on their pale, thin bodies. The woman didn't shout at me or curse me. Her eyes held a helpless expression. The children, scratching their necks, looked at me with sad eyes as if they expected me to perform a miracle on them. It was their expectancy which really terrified me. I backed off and ran away, leaving my things behind. I never returned to that market again to sell anything.

Soon afterwards I left that company and began selling for another organization which manufactured medicines for expelling stomach worms. My luck with them was no better. The products were aimed at both adults and children. I got more money than before, and a higher rate of commission. I asked no questions about the manufacture of the product and never tried it on myself. The job was a kind of graduation for me. I did quite well, till the old cycle began to catch up with me again. I had changed my sales approach, given myself a new name, almost a new identity, but it turned out that the medicines I sold for getting rid of worms in the stomach were so powerful that a child practically excreted its own intestines. A woman I had never seen before came to me and started dragging me up and down the garage saying that I had apparently poisoned her child. People ran up to me from nowhere and set upon me saying that I had killed their relations. I managed to escape from the murderous rage of those people by what I can only consider to be undeserved good fortune.

The medicines I sold also turned out to have rather bizarre side-effects. People came back complaining that the medicines made their hair fall out, that it rotted their teeth and made their skin start to flake. Others complained that the medicines stopped their bowel movements altogether. Some said it made them lose weight drastically; some that it made them fatter. I encountered a man who said that instead of getting rid of his stomach worms the medicine had begun to make him grow taller. Then it began to deform his bones. A woman complained that it had made her breasts shrink. I began to suspect that people were inventing their ailments, or that they took too many cheap drugs, or that they simply wanted to attach their problems to something because no one would listen to them anyway.

I finally decided I would no longer sell medicines that were trying to cure people of anything. The more they set out to cure, the more problems they seemed to create. But the truth was that, as there were so few jobs available, the only sales jobs to be obtained were ones that sold products which had to do with cures. Everybody seemed to need a cure for something. So, against my will, I had to adjust my resolve.

I first became aware of the persistence of my nightmares when I met my new boss. He ran a small drugs manufacturing company called CURES UNLIMITED. He had his two-room offices in a patch of land between the Ajegunle ghetto and the Apapa suburbs. He was a squat man, with an ugly face, and small alert eyes. He was as corpulent in body as I found him later to be thin on scruples. He always carried a fan of peacock feathers and wore faded agbada and slippers. He chewed kola nuts regularly. He had a team of unemployed graduates of science and medicine who manufactured the drugs in a secret laboratory near his house. He had a bevy of artists who designed the packets and came up with logos. He wrote his own selling lines. He had a secretary, who looked as if she never ate, and who spent most of her time peering into a small mirror. He had a sales force of five men.

My new boss could be called a man of our times. He understood the spirit of city business. He began from nothing. He too had sold patent medicines and graduated to manufacturing new tablets for headaches by mixing existing ones in the business. Like me, he had suffered his share of selling medicines that flaked people's skins and affected their reproductive abilities. He was, he assured me, interested only in bringing health to the battered people of the nation. What impressed me about my boss was that he insisted on members of the company using the medicines the company produced. Every morning when the workers arrived he made sure everyone had a spoonful of his drugs before they set out on the day's endeavour.

I worked happily with my new boss for a while. I was impressed with his ambitious attitude towards his drugs. I had been sufficiently drilled by starvation in the city to know how to sell anything. One secret is to assign the drugs an incredible multiplicity of functions. But with my new boss when I did this I was merely telling the truth as I knew it. I am not sure how much I was prepared for this condition by the swallowing of his drugs every morning. One of the medicines that my boss invented was called Koboko. Apparently it cured ring-worm, eczema, stomach upsets, malaria, yellow fever and headaches. It got rid of spots and pimples, it preserved youth, increased sexual virility, and provided continuous energy through the hot and bustling Lagos days. It was an all-purpose drug, and I never heard any complaints of strange side-effects. It was clear to us that our boss was revolutionizing the drugs business. Our sales team were very popular. Our drugs were bought in good quantities. And sometimes, by creating an artificial scarcity, we brought in surprisingly excellent profits on the days when we were bold enough to auction our drugs to the highest bidders.

I should have been happy. For the first time in my sales life my conscience was clear. But then one weekend, suddenly, my nightmares broke out on me, like an irrepressible rash from within. That was when I first realized that I had been living with them a long time without really knowing. After that weekend I couldn't sleep without being assaulted by a ferocious wave of nightmares. It got so bad I had become afraid of falling asleep at night. This began to affect my work, for I began to sleep in the daytime. I would be on the molue buses, my colleagues would be expecting me to begin my talk so they could rush up to me and buy the drugs, but I would be fast asleep on the seat, my head resting on the mass-ive shoulders of a market-woman. I became known, amongst my name-making colleagues, as the sleeping salesman. The news of this got to my boss and only served to make him force-feed me more of his drugs. They worked. They kept me awake during the day, they filled me with strange energies, odd inspirations, but at night they left me more vulnerable to the mercilessness of my dreams.

My nightmares were never quite the same. They were often, however, variations on a single theme. The earliest nightmare I remember began with me seeing that all I had ever sold in the way of medicines resulted in the deaths of thousands of children. I would be wandering aimlessly along the devastated streets of a Lagos bathed in lurid lights. Everywhere I turned I saw children drinking medicines as they played on the roadsides. I would become lost in a labyrinth: I would come to a crossroad, take a turning, and would see children clutching my bottles of medicines, dying on the roads. The smell of burning tar, and charred flesh, came from them, as if the medicines were acids that dissolved their insides. I saw children hallucinating and going mad in the forests. I saw their bodies piled on the backs of trucks. Everywhere I went people regarded me with strange eyes. I came to another crossroad where an albino child had bundles of my medicines. When the boy saw me he shouted. People came running. They pursued me with machetes. I ran till I was exhausted. When I fell the people bore down on me. They began beating me as I woke up. In another dream the scene would change. I would be in the corner of a nameless constellation, a lunar landscape where the dead sang and provided music. The stars in the sky were the objects of the auctioneer's block. One after another the stars were sold off. When a star was bought its light would go out. The singing would increase in sweetness. The auctioneer would sometimes be my boss – squat, monocled, drinking endless bottles of Guinness while he sold off the stars. Sometimes the auctioneer would be an old woman whom I had sold my medicines to on a molue bus. And other times the auctioneer would be a white man with a bent telescope.

When the stars were being auctioned I would realize with a shock that the people who bought them paid either with huge sums of money, a special part of the human anatomy, or the decapitated heads of newly-dead children. When the day's proceedings were over, when the lights had dimmed in the firmament, the auctioneer would look at the moon through a huge spy-glass, would laugh, and mutter:

'One day! One day!'

The singing would stop. The auctioneer would turn to me with strange eyes and would point at me. I would immediately be bound and thrown on the block. The auctioneer would bang on the table with a large fibula. Voices would rise from the darkness: the drunken voices of the rich. The auctioneer would invite the money-men of the high constellation to proceed with the naming of their prices for me, the nameless and underfed salesman who would sell anything. This was the part of the nightmare which continued every night and whose incredible variations always left me bewildered in the mornings. The money-men of the high constellation would crowd forward. They were representatives of all races, all nations, all colours. They had bloated faces, indifferent eyes. Their expressions were acutely wise and callous about the resources and the costs of power. They would screw up their eyes at me. I saw the face of an army general, an English aristocrat, an Asian millionaire, an American tycoon. (The rich belong to one country.) I saw the pinched face of a Yoruba chief, his agbada made from the skin of antelopes. I saw a senator whom I remembered coming to canvass votes in the ghetto of Ajegunle. (He had brought with him three truckloads of free dried milk. The women came rushing to his campaign truck, struggling for dried milk which would later poison them.) The senator had red and bulbous eyes. He stared at me vengefully. He had feathers sticking from his collar. During one of my dreams he began the auctioning by naming a miserable price. The proceedings grew in rowdiness. With the second bang of the fibula on the table someone, whom I never saw, offered a thousand naira for my head. Another offered ten cows. A third offered the heads of three children who had come first in their respective classes. A fourth offered the thighs of a famous wrestler who had disappeared in mysterious circumstances. The army general offered a machine for making money – a machine secretly approved by the nation's cabal of power. The voices rose, became noisy, and I would lose touch with the subsequent offers. The singing of the dead grew louder in my ears. I would begin to scream. The auctioneer would knock me out with the fibula. I would wake up to find many sweaty faces grinning closely at me. When I looked round I saw only faces, large blown-up faces smeared with antimony. The auctioneer would bang the table again. I had been sold.

The crowd of the rich would rise and start clapping. I never knew whom I had been sold to, or at what price. After the clapping had ceased I would hear a flourish of drums. The crowd would come towards me. Then a procession of women singing dirges, bearing clothes of twinkling lace materials in their arms, would surround me. They undressed me, washed me with the medicines I sold, then they would dress me up in the new clothes. As they led me from the constellation to a familiar world the sunlight would cut through the holes in the zinc ceiling and would burn a copper coin in the middle of my forehead.

The nightmares became so unbearable that it was necessary to do something about them. I went to the Celestial Church near where I lived and I had the priests pray over me; but the nightmares merely went on to include the priests, the members of the congregation, and biblical personages amongst the auctioneers. My nightmare became a hole which swallowed up my experiences, which absorbed the faces of all those to whom I turned for help. It got so bad that on a given day I couldn't tell whether I was in real life or in one of my dreams. Like all sensible and secretive Lagosians, I began to consult with herbalists and sorcerers. My colleagues recommended one to me. He was a herbalist who had his shack under a bridge and lived a roving existence, carrying his charms and potions to different parts of the city. I went to visit him and as soon as I entered his shack he announced that a terrible evil eye was on me. He blindfolded me, led me in, and told me of how my jealous colleagues had put spells on me, of how strange women had cursed me for the wrong I had done them. He raised such terrors in me that I almost went insane with paranoia. After making me pay him forty naira, and the price of two kola nuts, a bottle of ogogoro, and three chickens, he said, with inspired energy:

'I love bad dreams! I enjoy eating them! Give me all your nightmares! I am a collector. They make me strong. Give me all your nightmares this very minute!'

He grabbed my hands, filled them with a bundle of coarse leaves and alligator pepper seeds, and made me chew them, then made me mould them in my palm. Then he very roughly took them from me, whipped off the blindfold and blew a handful of ground peppers into my eyes. I screamed.

'Open your eyes and see!' he shouted.

I couldn't. He led me to the back of the shed and, with my eyes burning, he made me strip naked and bathe in boiling water to which was added baby's urine. Then he gave me a rag to dry myself with and sent me on my way. For three days I couldn't open my eyes properly. And for a few weeks afterwards my nightmares stopped. Then slowly my eyes opened to the madness I had been living with all those years.

The Salesman of Nightmares

Two weeks after seeing the herbalist I went off happily to work. I had slept soundly and dreamlessly. Ever since my visit not only had my nightmares stopped, but I had ceased dreaming altogether. One morning I woke up feeling unusually light, but also with the distinct sensation that I had seen some bats flying into my room through cracks in the wooden window. I ransacked my room, but found nothing. I went to the bathroom to have a wash and discovered, as if for the first time, that the rubbish dump in the backyard had grown so high that it was impossible to see the forest. I grumbled to my neighbours and they grumbled back at me. After bathing I left for the office to collect my medicines for the day's sales. When my boss saw me he called me into his office. He was in an unusually expansive mood.

'My friend, Arthur,' he said, smiling broadly, 'We have just successfully manufactured the perfect money-making medicine!'

'Is that true?' I asked.

He got up from his seat. He banged on his table and called in his secretary. When she came in he sent her to go and buy two bottles of Guinness. When she had gone he came round the table. He seemed quite overcome with excitement. He kept playing with the bunch of gold-plated chains round his neck. Then he picked up his fan of peacock feathers, and said:

'Just imagine, my sleeping salesman, the medicine that can cure insomnia, VD, syphilis, that can increase your height, that can help you put on weight or lose it, that will put a sparkle in your eyes, a medicine full of vitamins and iron, that can improve your complexion, that can get rid of stomach worms, that can make you last longer in bed, that is good for children, and which can give you three times more energy than anything else we have manufactured to date.'

He looked at me expectantly. I didn't know what to

97

say. I had been fairly overloaded with information. He continued:

'Well, we have it now. One of our boys went to India to get the patent. But we added a few things of our own. The first batch came in today.'

The secretary returned with two bottles of stout.

'Shall I open both of them, sir?'

'No! What's wrong with you?'

She opened one bottle and left. My boss, fanning himself, turned to me.

'You won't believe how powerful the medicine is. I have taken it myself and it works wonders. Three women I have had today. Three!'

He went behind his table and brought out samples from a drawer and gave me three yellow boxes with a crude painting of a musclebound wrestler, a generalized face of a beautiful African woman, and a child. The name of the medicine, POWER-DRUG, was written in red letters on all six sides of the box. And all over, on every available space, were the names of all the ailments the medicine cured. It read like a complete list of the illnesses and afflictions of the poor. Inside the boxes were little round translucent bottles with green liquids in them. My boss tried to get me to drink some, but I refused. He worked himself into a temper, reminded me of all the things he had done for me, and threatened me with the sack. I swallowed a spoonful. It tasted like a combination of mint and bitterleaves. Nothing happened.

'You wait,' he said, calming down.

He went and sat at his chair and stared at me grimly from behind his table. He looked quite ugly, with his face of a strange English dog, his flat nose, small eyes, small head, and thick neck. On the walls there were almanacs and calendars and pull-outs from cheap magazines showing bare-breasted women in startling positions of undress. There were also framed certificates of licences to manufacture and there were diplomas in salesman-ship and chemistry from colleges I had never heard of, or ever known to have existed. His table was crowded with business cards, pens, unopened letters, a list of pharma-ceutical companies, a book on chemistry, a dictionary of symptoms, a small encyclopaedia of medicine which he had bought from a salesman and which he had never read, a table-fan which never worked, empty bottles of stout, pills, boxes of aspirin and cough medicines, and a telephone which wasn't connected. After a while of staring at me, awaiting my response, he said:

'Well?'

'Excellent!' I said. 'Powerful!'

He smiled. His expansive mood returned. He clapped his hands, got up, opened the big boxes behind his office door, and gave me fifty bottles of POWER-DRUG along with the usual numbers of pills, tubes, bottles of unguents and vitamins for all the numerous ailments which drove Lagosians, day after livid day, to listen to our sales talks on buses, at street corners, at garages, marketplaces, and part with their hard-earned money. The truth is that my boss knows the city. I had begun to accept that there had to be something effective about our drugs for people to buy them again and again with no complaints. In a voice of startling volume, my boss said:

'Arthur, our sleeping salesman, wake up and listen!'

I nodded. In a louder voice, waving his fan of peacock feathers in the air, spreading his arms so that his agbada made him look like a squat, monstrous bird, he said:

'We are launching this one with a mighty bang! I want you to sell like a madman, sell as if your life depended on it. I want you to create such an impression, whip up the public's interest, till the whole city is queuing outside our office fighting for this new medicine. Do you understand me? I am assigning two more people on your route. They will build up to your talk. I want you to use your entire range of sales tricks. Take another spoonful of medicine. That's right. When the power enters you they will see for themselves. As you do your sales talk keep taking the medicine. Let them see it working on you. Today I want you to come back empty-handed. There will be a bonus for the highest seller.'

He glared at me and began to fan himself. He drank deeply from his bottle of Guinness. Then he picked up the telephone receiver and very loudly called in his secretary.

'What are you doing sitting there?' he said to me when he put the phone down.

'Go out and sell! Go out and multiply!'

The secretary came in. I went out.

The day began badly. The molue buses, with their unstable bodywork, were too full. People were jammed all the way up the aisles. Children on their way to school, market-women with their bundles of goods, people off to work, were crammed in every available space of the buses. Even the doorways were packed with people clinging on, as if their sanity depended on it. There was just simply no space for us to get up and do our sales talk. Me and my two colleagues had to sit in a bukka, drinking hot beer, waiting for the rush-hour to pass. It was just one of those days. The rush hour seemed to go on for ever. We decided, after a few beers, to go ahead with our sales anyway. If we waited for the buses to empty out a little we would never get started. It was very hot and the beer made me drowsy. I sat in the bukka, preparing to move, but my eyes shut, my head drooped, and in a velvet instant I felt myself falling into a void. At the bottom of the void there was a still, green sea. Someone tapped me on the shoulder. I stood up.

'Let's go,' I said.

We got onto the first molue bus that came along. It was as crowded as ever. We were like refugees escaping from a bombed city. It was boiling hot on the bus and everyone sweated on everyone else. Children strapped to their mother's backs were crushed and they kept wailing. The passengers bore the overcrowding with bad-tempered noisiness. The bus stank of sweat and dried fish. It was impossible to escape the undernourishment of the children. When passengers clambered off at their various stops, when the bus cleared a bit, the man who was supposed to build up to my sales act was forestalled by someone. I was very irritated. We went slowly over the bridge spanning the lagoon. Green and still. In the brightness of noon the water was a ripple of blinding metal. The smell of excrement wafted in through the window and one of the passengers said we had just passed the area of the lagoon where they emptied some of the nightsoil of the city.

The man who had forestalled my colleague, and who talked volubly, was foreign to us. He had long, trailing, matted hair, over which was a knitted hat of red, green, and gold. People speculated that he was some sort of nationalist. Others said he was a new kind of preacher. He reminded me of dishevelled biblical prophets. He spoke in an accent which none of us understood at first. One of the women on the bus said she had seen him at the Independence Square denouncing African leaders, shouting that Africa had been betrayed, and that he preached a strange religion with an Ethiopian as the new Jesus. Some people laughed at this. A student said that he was a Rastafarian. Some people made fun of the name. But the Rastafarian went on preaching. He said we were selling our souls, our power, to white capitalists. He talked about Jah's inviolable fire. He said, in a dramatic voice that kept us quiet:

'Africa! We counting on yuh!'

He began to sour my day. He continued:

'Africa! It's a lang time since di disintegrashion of our dreams and many years after hindipendence white people dem still fuck us up! Africa, we counting on yuh!'

'Count yourself,' someone said.

The Rastafarian turned towards the person who had spoken and launched into a long speech. As he progressed he got more vigorous. There seemed no chance of stopping him. He spoke torrentially, spicing it with snatches of songs. The passengers, never missing a chance to praise a good singer, clapped for him. During the pause a Jehovah's Witness got up and began to preach of Armageddon. I grew more and more enraged.

I kept signalling to my colleagues, but they were too involved in the drama. The Rastafarian declaimed louder, riding over the apocalyptic speech of the Jehovah's Witness.

'Africa awake! Jah call yuh to glory!'

He paused for breath. I took the opportunity to launch, without preparation, into my sales act. I said, loudly, in a nasal accent I had long perfected:

'The man wey cross River Niger with bicycle don come-o!'

The passengers cheered.

'The man wey no deh talk politics when people never chop don come-o!'

They cheered again.

I proceeded to denounce the Jehovah's Witness. Then I said I had never heard of Jah and had they? The passengers said they hadn't. Then I told them that there was a new drug in the country which could cure ninety percent of the illnesses of our people. I rushed out an impressive list, adding along the way a couple of new diseases which the moment invented for me. I said the medicine had been produced with the co-operation of the most important pharmaceutical companies in the world. I said that because it was so powerful the drug was originally too expensive. I told them that our company had decided to produce it cheaply so that all the people in Lagos who were as poor as I was (they laughed) could afford it. I passed samples around so they could look at it, feel its healing powers, taste the sense of possession for a fleeting second. I said that the drug was more effective than anything the white man had invented. I said this was the product of African powers, the collaboration of Africa and India. I made extraordinary claims for it; I said it could cure anything from headaches to elephantiasis, that they could either drink it, bathe with it, rub it on their skin, or sniff its essences in boiling water. I said it was good for children and old people, that it gave more power, more iron, than any existing drug. When I made my talk in English, I spoke other versions in seven different national languages. Then I opened a bottle and drank a little from it: I sang: I span riddles and proverbs. An inspired energy took hold of my brain. To my greatest surprise the Rastafarian came forward, took a sample, paid for it, opened the bottle, sniffed the contents and, muttering something about it being the work of Jah's children in Africa, bought three other bottles off me. I was astonished. He opened a bottle and frightened me by drinking down half the contents.

That was all the galvanizing the passengers needed: the endorsement of a stranger. If I had planned it the whole event couldn't have worked out better. Suddenly people began coming forward. One of them bought two bottles, another bought five, a woman bought four. The excitement became a little uncontrollable. People began to struggle and rush. Anyone might have thought I was selling a rare elixir. It was as if, in an instant, and totally by surprise, they had come across the answers to all their problems. They brought their money from innumerable recesses and secret pockets. The market-women loosened their wrapper-ends or dug deep into the pouches they had hidden in the folds of their clothes. They paid with notes so crumpled and crushed that it took minutes to unfold them and ascertain that those pieces of paper were indeed acceptable currencies.

The bus-conductor, a man full of dark, nervous energies, whom I had become familiar with on my various trips, bought two bottles. The driver, who had wild eyes and a slash across his face which actually made him rather handsome, bought three bottles. The passengers cleared my entire stock. I had only a few samples left, which I chose to keep for myself. I began to sell the pills and tubes of lesser medicines. They went with the flood of interest in POWER-DRUG.

The molue bus was clamorous with bawling children and hawkers noisily selling their wares to passengers through the open windows. The bus-conductor told me that the driver had imbibed most of the contents of a bottle and thought that it was even better as alcohol than it was as a drug.

'I' hear that you people sometimes put whisky and marijuana in these drugs,' the conductor said to me conspiratorially.

'It's a lie!' I said, vehemently.

The Rastafarian seized on the furore to criticize African leaders who ignored the sufferings of their own people. He said that our Heads of States had illegally enriched themselves and their supporters while the people died for lack of basic amenities.

We got to a bus-stop and the clamour increased as people fought to get off and as others struggled to get on. Eventually the bus began to move, and the traffic eased on over the bridge. We passed some traffic policemen, who looked a little sickly in their yellow uniform tops.

My colleagues came over and suggested that we get back
to the office and collect some more drugs to sell. I agreed.
The bus sped on. Voices rose. We heard the protestations of the engine as the vehicle changed gear. We also
heard the driver singing. It was only when we noticed
that another molue was speeding alongside us, with
both drivers challenging each other, that we realized we
were engaged in an absurd war of wills. The conductor
joined in the contest, spurring his driver on, urging him
not to allow the other molue driver – 'a bushman from
Abeokuta' – to overtake us. The conductor, intoxicated
with the contest, recited the entire list of the driver's
nicknames:

'Omo-Shango, Omo-Egba, Master of the Road, Cap-
tain Blood, Omo-Lorry, Don't let that bastard overtake
us-o!'

The driver accelerated maniacally. He changed gear
with such dramatic flourish, such energy, I feared he
would wrench the gear from its socket. The driver, trying
to prevent the other molue from compounding his
victory by getting right in front of us, changed gears
again with an even more vigorous flourish. The change
of gear sounded like a deep tubercular cough. The driver
ran our vehicle close to the other one. The bus-
conductors of both vehicles urged their drivers on,
chanting names and songs. At first the passengers
entered into the spirit of the contest. But the cranking of
the gears, the deep cough of the engine, began to scare
us. I banged on the ceiling of the bus and shouted that
the driver should take it easy. The passengers joined me
in shouting. But the driver pressed on with demented

euphoria at the race, taking occasional sips from POWER-DRUG. In an instant, during which a glint of demonic obsession appeared in the driver's face, I realized that, without knowing it, I had become a salesman of nightmares. When the Rastafarian rose again (staggering, slurring his words) to tell us that we were all in the hands of the fiery Jah, his hat fell off with his dreadlocks. At the same moment, the bus rammed against the railings of the bridge, ran over pavement and metal, and lost control.

The passengers wailed and set up a cacophony that made everything worse. The molue ran up against the last railings, and forced its way through. The conductor disappeared. The passengers began to jump out of the windows. There was screaming and fighting, confused people running everywhere, tripping over bundles, trapped in their seats, clinging to their neighbours. A child screamed in the midst of the crush. From where I stood, with my briefcase under my arms, trapped by the tide of people, separated from my colleagues, I saw women scampering here and there, I saw the rashes of ringworm on bared backs, I saw the heads of children squashed against the metalwork of the vehicle. I saw pickpockets squeezing money from the mad situation. I saw the Rastafarian fighting his way through, in his hand his fake dreadlocks attached to his hat. I tried to jump out of the window. With my eyes on fire, my brain boiling over with terrible potencies, I saw the lagoon as a corrugated sheet of frosted green glass. Then I realized that the vehicle was perched between the air and the bridge. I ran the other way, to the section that was on the bridge. The Rastafarian was in front of me, railing, praying aloud. He wouldn't rush on ahead and he wouldn't get out of the way. I shoved him aside and reached a window. I was about to jump out when he caught me by the back of my shirt.

'Fucking drug,' he said.

I knocked his hand off and suddenly felt the bus going over. I heard a multitude of voices lift to the heavens. As the bus fell I jumped out of the window. I thought the concrete would rise to anchor me on firm ground. For a moment I saw nothing but sky. Then I saw the city tumbling, turning, upside down. I saw the bridge spinning above me. I heard the molue splash mightily into the lagoon. The air rushed up to me. Then a surge of green water rose to pluck me from the air. After a while I surfaced and steadied myself. The molue had sunk. I saw a few heads bobbing on the water. I fought the tide and swam ashore. I found that I was near the area where the nightsoil was dumped into the lagoon. Helpers arrived by the multitude. As always in these kinds of accidents the driver and the conductor survived. I learnt later on that only seven people drowned.

Escape to the Town of Scandals

I can note all this now with a certain serenity. At the time my head was continually on fire. I couldn't sleep for days. I didn't return home for a week. I kept having visions of the police pouncing on me. I didn't read the papers and I roved about the city, staying under bridges, snatching rest under the open sky. Then one afternoon I went back to my room, gathered my belongings, and dumped them at an uncle's place. I went to the bank and withdrew as much of my money as my mean-minded bank would allow. With bats buzzing in my head, I went to Iddo garage. Without thinking I took a Peugeot taxi for the town of W. where I had spent the best part of my adolescence learning about survival.

Yes, I can note all this now with a certain serenity. But the nightmares returned with greater ferocity and it kept knocking through my head that I was responsible for the accident and the deaths of seven people. As I left the city I carried with me not only the world of jostling market-women, teeming undernourished children, the short-tempered unemployed, the brusque faces of pickpockets, I also carried some bottles of POWER-DRUG with the hope that I might run across someone who could isolate its dangerous components.

The Peugeot that took me to the town of W. drove so fast I was convinced that the accident I had escaped in the city would befall me on the open roads. The driver shot down the hairpin turns, the narrow bridges, as if he were insane, as if he had a special appointment with death. The more I pleaded with him to go gently the faster he went. When one of the passengers whispered to me that the driver looked doped to the eyeballs, I resigned myself to my fate. We passed several victims of accidents on the way: cars that had run into iroko trees; cars that had sped over bridges, with blood on the rocks below; lorries that had crashed into one another, entang-led, their engines still purring; vehicles that had overturned. My escape from the city was like a journey through nightmares.

We arrived in W. late in the evening. The car shot past the school where I had grown up. It was with some relief that I saw the fields, the goal-posts, and the principal's house. The name of the school had changed. I learnt later that it had become a lot more respectable. It used to be the classic school for those who were to study in their lives the crude mythologies of survival.

When we arrived at the town's garage I went and booked myself into a cheap hotel which held memories for me of my school days. The hotel was seedier than I remembered. There were flies everywhere. The red paint was peeling from the walls. The fans moved slowly and the heat was unbearable. From my room I could smell the toilets. The food was terrible. In the lounge downstairs, which served as a dance-floor in the evenings, music poured out from abysmal loudspeakers. There were old men around, earthbound sailors who had glimpsed Gibraltar through a spray of booze, and who talked intermittently about Katanga and about their time in the Congo when they were soldiers. There were middle-aged prostitutes around as well. They had acquired predatory grins and they danced sensually. There were no young women. I washed, ate, and drank three bottles of beer. I tried to sleep, but the nightmares kept riding over me, pouring over me, washing away any possibility of rest. The mosquitoes in the room drove me to paroxysms of helplessness. So I got dressed again and wandered from night-club to night-club in the hope of finding some of my old schoolmates.

It was with some shock that I realized that W. was such a small town. I had always thought of it as a centre of excitement and scandal. In fact it was a town with a history of slave-trading, a town of bad dreams, surrounded by creeks and forests of palm-trees and rubber plantations. It had become a centre of excitement only on account of its abundance of oil wells. At all the night-clubs the youths dressed in the latest importations of American fashion. Everyone spoke with a curious transatlantic accent. When I asked people about the best place to spend the night they told me that the Boom Night-club was the centre of the town's sophisticated night-life.

I went there. There was an indifferent band playing. Strobe-lights revolved on the green walls. There were prostitutes everywhere. They looked startlingly pretty at first glance. I drank steadily, intensely. That night it turned out to be my misfortune to find what I was seeking. I met two of my old schoolmates. When I saw Takwa and Amukpe something happened in me. I felt the bats' return. My friends saw me and stared, remembering. Then Takwa burst out laughing. He shouted my name and came over and shook my hand for a long time. Amukpe slapped me on the back and took to mentioning my nicknames, singing old school songs, coming out with snatches of nostalgia. They both insisted that I joined them where they were sitting. Then they both went off to buy a table-full of drinks.

Takwa was now a schoolteacher. His father, before him, had also been a teacher. Takwa's children will be teachers. Some people have a greater dynastic sense than others. At school he used to compose precious letters to just about everybody, from the Queen of England to the Headmistress of the Catholic girls school near our college. He used to be the perfect toady to the children of the rich. He was their servant. He coached them before every examination. He organized women for them. In return they took care of his feeding, his pocket-money, his holidays, his clothes.

Amukpe was a menial worker at an oil rig. He had dropped out of school in his fourth year. Working in an oil rig meant he earned more money than those who went on to university. He made up for the fact that he had dropped out of school by living as lavishly as possible. He was another toady to the children of the rich. He covered up for them when they were wrong, he took their punishments for them, washed their clothes, took their beatings and insults, sided with them in all arguments and got to know their families. He was an inveterate gambler who would go on for days without food because he had lost his rations on the tumble of dice. He used to sneak out through the barbed-wire fences of the school at night to watch westerns, to attend dances, to pursue girls. It was a wonder how he passed the exams he did, though it was no secret that he was helped by the rich who were often able to buy examination questions in advance.

When they came back to the table, laughing, their arms loaded with beer, I realized that it was a mistake to have escaped to W. Amongst other things, it was a town where you had to have something to show for yourself. If you didn't you were considered a failure and you would be greatly avoided. I had nothing to show for myself but a dog-eared collection of sales correspondence, a few useless certificates in salesmanship, a briefcase full of weird drugs, a head teeming with bats, and a vision of a bus disappearing into the green lagoon.

My schoolmates told me a lot of stories, updating old scandals. Then they began to ask me questions about myself. They asked what I was doing, how I earned my living, and whether I had gone to university. Decorum compelled me to lie. As a salesman, embellishing lies comes naturally. I told them that I was a manager with ICI and that I had two degrees. I said my car had been involved in an accident and that I was on holiday recuperating. As I spoke they got nervous. I preened. I warmed to the fantasies. I played the part as thoroughly as the town of W. demands. I added that after my holiday I was going to the United States of America. They must have hated my guts. To say, in W., that one is going to America is like saying one is visiting the moon. The town of W. revolves, amongst its youths, around dreams of escape. Everyone is stretched between being a nobody and going to America.

The conversation, after these revelations, turned a little sour. No one in W. likes being upstaged. Takwa went and got more drinks. Amukpe was silent all the time he was gone. When Takwa got back they both began to talk about our schooldays. Takwa, the writer of precious letters which never got replies, beamed at me and asked if I had ever heard from Odeh. The question made me uncomfortable. Suddenly I became aware of how bad the music was: a brash, irritating jangle of drums and guitars. The revolving lights made my eyes feel funny. I felt as if I were in a bottle of green liquid. Takwa had, with the seemingly innocent stroke of which the town of W. makes you a master, cracked the bottle open. Both of them began to laugh rather heartily. I tried not to remember. But sitting in the night-club, with the band pouring out awful music, with people milling around in the strobe-lights, a few dancing (everyone in W. prides themself on being the best dancer in the country), with a few men struggling over women (every public event revolves round 'capturing' women), and with two men fighting near the bar, I could not prevent my memories from breaking on me. I was wrenched back to that year at school, my final year, when I was tied to a tree, stoned with rotten oranges, and made to count the stars for three days.

The Children of Curfew-makers

There I was, on inter-college sports day, the most wretched student of our generation. I was badly dressed. I had stolen someone else's shorts and they were too big for me. My shirt was in tatters. Everything was bright that day. The fields had been closely-cropped by punished truants. The sun gleamed on the green leaves. The school buildings had been freshly painted. I remember being overcome with the smell of newly-cut grass. Expensively dressed girls from other colleges were all around: sports was our love dance. All the boys were chatting up girls. Takwa became famous that year for successfully seducing three different girls from the Catholic school.

I was standing besides the goal-post when Odeh came up to me. He was as tall as a ladder, and as thin. He was the eldest son of one of the town's richest men. His father, it was widely believed, made his money from armed robbery and then invested wisely. In our time everyone makes their money with a broad touch of the criminal. Odeh walked up to me, beaming. I had helped him in numerous examinations. He was my financial protector, depending on his mood. He was extraordinarily well-dressed. He wore linen shorts, a silk shirt, a bright yellow waistcoat (made in England), red socks and white shoes. He held a gold-bordered handkerchief in his hand. A bundle of pound notes showed from his shirt-pocket. If it was the day of love dances, he was the chief peacock.

When he got to where I was standing he asked me to deliver a letter to a certain girl. She turned out to be the daughter of one of the richest men in Benin, a bigger pond than the town of W. I was apprehensive. But Odeh bore down on me, threatened me with the withdrawal of his patronage and protection, and made me feel like a confirmed wretch straight out of Dickens. He was the rich man's son and I was the goal-post. I had no choice. I took the letter and went towards the girl. She stood a short distance away, chattering with a coterie of female toadies. But before I got there Assi intercepted me. He was also the son of a rich man, the other richest man in town. Without any preamble he gave me a letter to the same girl and he also gave me ten pounds. To buy me off. Odeh strode towards me, snatched the ten-pound note out of my hands, tore it to shreds, gave me fifty pounds, and pushed me on my way. And so it went. That was how I became a victim of their financial contest. Between them they managed to tear up two hundred pounds.

Naturally this attracted a great deal of attention. People crowded round us, and watched the obscene spectacle. The competition between the two boys – Odeh was tall, Assi was short and fat – soon mirrored the endless financial contests between their parents. In one year Odeh's father, at an important public dance, was declared the richest man in town. The next year, at another significant event, Assi's father was declared winner. If one of them bought a Rolls Royce the other would buy two. If one of them imported a Citroen Special the other would import the same, but with more ostentatious gadgets. The women who came into the orbits of these two families had to take a stand. People were frequently suspected of being spies for the other camp. Women were often seduced from one household to the other. Wives were sometimes snatched. And the town of W., with all of its real and manufactured excitements, had the bitter feuds of the two disgustingly rich families added to it.

I remember the year at school when both men were invited to chair an important fund-raising function. The school needed to raise money for the building of an assembly hall. They could not invite one man without inviting the other. Odeh's father opened with a speech vaguely denouncing his rival. He spoke very badly. Like most of the rich, he was a complete illiterate. When the speech was over he waved to his men. They carried over a white sack. Then he began to toss money from the platform. He threw coins and pound notes at the crowd as if money were nothing but a cheap magician's trick. The students went wild struggling to pick up the scattered money. When Assi's father's turn came he signalled to his musicians and they piped the organs, strummed their guitars, and squeezed vaguely familiar tunes from their accordions. When they had finished he made a long speech, devoid of denunciations (it hadn't come to that yet) and presented a cheque for ten thousand pounds to the school. The teachers and the principal privately declared Assi's father the winner of that contest. We the students, beneficiaries of coins and crumpled pound notes, declared that Odeh's father had won. At the time these contests, which affected every sphere of life in W., were like a fiction to us. We didn't wholly believe that they were real, that adults went around doing things of that nature. Time was to teach us that those who get on in society, those who rise high and affect events, do so by manipulating, by manufacturing, reality.

And so it was that I found myself caught in the middle of the mirror images of their parents' insanities. Some of the sports events had to be held up because of the interest generated by Odeh and Assi trying to buy the other out. Some of my classmates, inveterate hustlers, had begun their own side bets. When the two rich boys got around to tearing up another hundred pounds I had to shout at them to stop. I took the money that they had torn up, pocketed the shreds, and told them that the best man would win. Caught in a situation where I had effectively been bought by both of them, a prisoner to the freshness of their money, I staggered off to the girl and took her aside.

She was the prime female peacock. She wore shoes made in France, a light poncho, a pair of pearl-studded jeans, and had a robin's feather in her hair. Apparently she had no idea that the whole spectacle had been taking place on account of her. I began with a rambling introduction of myself, in which I told her that I was in disguise and that my father was the governor of the state. A flame of interest momentarily lit up in her eyes. I told her a few jokes, asked her a riddle she couldn't answer, and I let it be known that I was the brightest student in the whole college and that I had won a federal scholarship. Now that I look back I am convinced that this was my earliest preparation for a life as a salesman. I sold myself fluently. She tried not to be too impressed with me, but when I told her to meet me in three hours time she gave me an almost imperceptible nod. I wrote out the address where we should meet (a friend's elder brother's place) and warned her to be careful of the two pompous sons of smalltown millionaires. She smiled at this remark.

I went back to the dwindling crowd around Odeh and Assi who were awaiting the outcome of the contest. I told them that the girl was so confused by all the interest in her that it was necessary for them to provide further proof of the seriousness of their intentions. They started to produce some more money, but I stopped them. I told them that she wanted a more intelligent proof, something that required effort worthy of their declared affection, something like a poem, or better still a letter.

'She wants both of you to write her a letter. The best letter wins,' I said.

Without wasting any time Odeh grabbed Takwa by the neck and dragged him off to the dormitories. Assi got hold of our English teacher and (it may be difficult to believe, but money has the smell of a million perfumes) bought him into writing his letter to the girl.

I was so wretched that I had everything to gain from all this. I went back to the dormitories, stuck together a good number of the torn pound notes, stole a motley collection of clothes belonging to other students, and had a bath. I managed to emerge looking quite decent. I went to the pitch and met the two parties. Their letters were ready. Takwa's letter, written in a fussy calligraphic hand, was perfumed and bordered with dried roses. It was quite short and it made three references to Shakespeare, one to the Bible, and four to an English thriller writer, who was the rage at the time, called James Hadley Chase. The English teacher's letter was very long and over-perfumed. It made seven references to the Shakespeare of Romeo and Juliet and King Lear, three to Jane Austen, six to someone we had never heard of called Molière, five to Byron's Don Juan, and three to Shelley.

I went off with the letters and made my rendezvous on time to see her coming out of a limousine. I disappeared from my anxious colleagues and from school for weeks. I had the money. I burned the letters. And I made love to the girl in four different rooms in three cities. We wound up in her father's chalet on the edge of town. She was nothing special – all she wanted was flattery and excitement. I exhausted myself entertaining her. Making love to her was a poor compensation for all the effort, the energy and inventiveness it took to prevent her from being bored. The thought that I might end up entertaining her for a lifetime seemed more terrifying than dying of kwashiorkor or cholera. She was like a great insatiable void into which I poured my soul. I lost weight. I found her ennui insidious. One morning, to escape from her relentless demands to be entertained, I went to town and discovered that the police were searching for me. I went back to her father's chalet and made love to her again. She almost crushed the living daylights from my testicles with her excessive responsiveness. In the days that followed she talked of nothing but her summer shopping in Venice, Paris, and New York. She talked about the boredom of having to sit exams. Like Assi and Odeh, she had failed her examinations numerous times and it was only the weight of her father's contributions to various building projects of the Catholic school that made it possible for her to continue to be a student.

I became bored with her chatter. I wanted to escape her negation, the wearying tedium of her presence. It drained me to listen to her, to nod at her requests, laugh at her jokes, attend her every whim, be her clown, and to flatter her every action. Then one evening she surprised me by asking, as a sign of her affections, if I wanted the questions for the forthcoming School Certificate examinations. To please her, I said I would. I never recovered from my disappointment, from the casual, almost tender, shattering of my illusions. I took copies of the questions and in the morning I fled from her. I was going past our campus in a taxi when some followers of Odeh saw me. They gave chase, caught the cab in a traffic jam, dragged me out, and led me back to the dormitories where I was put on trial. I was, naturally, found guilty. They tied me to a tree and threw rotten oranges at me. I stayed there all night. Counting the stars. Re-counting them. It was only when I offered the group the questions of the forthcoming examinations that they let me go. But a few days later, at a night-club, I ran into Assi's gang. This time they competed as to who could wreak on me the most havoc. I counted stars for three days.

Nightmare, the Preparation for Ritual

Takwa and Amukpe, unaffected by the decibels, went on telling stories of my escapades. I went and bought my round of drinks. They moved on to talking about how our various schoolmates were doing. One was in jail for smuggling cocaine. Another had become a writer. A third was a footballer. There was one whom we all thought would go into the movies, but who now ran a brothel in Lagos. Another had been repatriated after trying to stow away on a ship bound for America. Odeh had become a lawyer. Rumour had it that he bought his degree from a phony college in England. Assi had also become a lawyer. He bought his degree as well. The feuds between the two families still existed. Every year at the important public dances they sprayed money and careful checks were kept by the town's thriving gossips as to how much was lavished. Takwa told me that the court case between the families, concerning a large tract of land, was still being fought. They had been pursuing the case for fifteen years. Both families had bought all the judges and magistrates in town, but there had been no Solomon to find a way out of the incredible deadlock.

My two schoolmates kept talking, kept reviewing the years. I sank deeper into despondency. Some girls came to join us and I perked up. Takwa and Amukpe kept trying to put me down. I was beginning to think of escaping from the night-club when Takwa said that the next public display of wealth was in a few days' time. The beer I had been drinking, manufactured by a brewery owned by Assi's father, had begun to stir the bats in my head. I rushed to the toilet and threw up. I returned stable, but rather miserable. The girls had shared themselves out. I had none. Takwa went on talking:

'This display will be the heaviest yet. If you attend there's no way you won't leave with hundreds of naira in your pocket. You must struggle though. You must swallow your dignity. Whether you are a manager or not it's an event you can't miss.'

I nodded.

Then he told me that Odeh was in town.

'He rides a Rolls Royce now.'

The bats in my head whispered that I should leave town, go back to Lagos, and find another job. I went on drinking, listening to their gossip. When my eyes got so blurred that I saw green people everywhere on the dance-floor, I decided to get back to the hotel. I was very drunk. When I got there I couldn't sleep. The prostitutes, all of them rather rough-looking, kept pestering me. When I finally did get some sleep a new variation of the nightmare came down on me. The auction was taking place not in a nameless constellation, but in the whole country. Parts of my body were being sold off. When someone bought a part of me the auctioneer would bang on the table. Odeh bought my arms. Assi inspected my feet and finally acquired them. The Rastafarian bought my ears. Takwa bought my eyes, and Amukpe my mouth. The auctioneer opened the floor for offers on a certain part of my anatomy. I screamed. A prostitute, dressed like a princess, came along, washed my testicles with kerosene, and was about to set fire to them when my boss stepped on to the stage. The prostitute withdrew. My boss said he had forgiven me for running away. He said that people really begin to understand how to make money when they are in trouble.

'The greater your crimes,' he said, 'the greater the risks you have to take.'

He told me that he had now opened a bigger company and I should become his chief salesman. I asked what I would be selling. He smiled and brought out a more finished version of POWER-DRUG. The colour of the liquid had changed. It was now the strange blue of certain acids. He gave me some to drink. I did, and began to dissolve. When I woke up in the morning six bats, in wing formation, flew out of the window. At first I thought they were angels.

The Manufacturers of Reality

Takwa came to see me at the hotel in the evening. He told me that he had managed to see Odeh and had come to take me to him. He warned me to be prepared for a few surprises. We took a taxi to the Oguso Lodge, home of Odeh's family. The building was palatial, resplendent with colonnades, balconies, statues. The house was hidden from the street by dense clusters of ferns, bougainvillaeas, and tropical flowers. There were ivies clasping the walls. The windows had rich brocaded curtains. Seven men stood guard at the gates, with big Alsatians between them. When we got there they phoned through to Odeh. He came to one of the balconies and waved us in. The main door was of cedarwood, heavy, imposing. The knocker on the door was fashioned in the shape of a fearsome warrior. Odeh let us into the most splendid house I had ever seen. The ceiling tinkled with chandeliers. There were stuffed parrots in three cages. The air-conditioner purred softly. There were mirrors on the walls. The settees were a gold colour. The tables were of blue glass. The floor was so richly carpeted that I walked on tiptoe. We went upstairs. There were massive photographs of Odeh's father in leopard-skin, shaking hands with people as diverse as the Head of State, the Prime Minister of England, and a Japanese businessman. The walls were lined with gourds, masks, and charms. The cured head of a lion stared down at us as we entered the main sitting-room. Further in there were masquerade outfits, surrounded with trailings. There were swords and daggers, shields

and sheaths, knives and guns in cabinets on the wall.
The room looked like a museum. It was unbelievably
spacious – there was no sense of crowding. In one corner
there was a rattan rocker, in another a hexagonal
Chippendale shelf. Elaborate bird cages, empty of birds,
hung everywhere. There were tables of iroko wood,
carved in shapes of warriors or elephants in meditation.
Odeh led us into the room and turned to me, smiling. He
had grown taller than could be reasonably expected. He
had also grown a beard. He looked like an elongated
image of his father.

'You're as short as ever,' he said, laughing. 'Some
people never grow.'

'And I need telescopes to see you,' I said.

He asked us to sit. We sat, gingerly, on the edge of the
settees. He did not sit, but towered over us. He spent the
whole time talking about himself. He offered us nothing
to drink. The sight of decanters, bottles of champagne
and whisky in the glass cabinet near us made us very
thirsty. He seemed rather dimly to remember me. He
didn't ask a single question about how we were doing.
He talked about his time in England and about all the
white girls he had gone out with. He fetched us his
awesome album of photographs and made us look
through. He talked about the company owned by his
father, of which he was now managing director, and
about the forthcoming financial contest and how they
were going to bury the town in money. While he
addressed us he kept shouting instructions to drivers,
servants, and bodyguards. The smell of excellent
cooking wafted up from the stairs and we salivated as he

talked, uninterrupted, for an entire hour. He only stopped when the sound of dancing and guttural voices came from the street. We went to the balcony and saw people fleeing in different directions on the street below.

The dancers looked fierce. They were muscled, with animal skins round their waists, feathers in their hair, charms round their necks, and weighted bangles on their arms. They all carried machetes, some had spears. Their faces were daubed with antimony, their bodies covered in native chalk and animal blood. The leader of the cultic dancers wore a rather terrifying gold-fringed lion head-dress. They held live chickens and danced vigorously in front of the house, chanting and clashing their machetes, with sparks flying. When Odeh made a sign to them with his fan the cultic dancers jumped, chanted something, bit off the heads of the chickens, and spat them on the ground. They danced wildly and let the chicken blood pour on them. The headless chickens flapped and the dancers weaved. At another sign from Odeh they dashed into the street, waving their machetes murderously. They tore after bicyclists, ran after children, pursued the women. In a few minutes the street was completely empty. The dancers had scattered everywhere, clanging their machetes on doors, scraping them on the tarmac, singing their fearful ritual songs.

Odeh told us that we should stay in the house till a special car came for us. I asked why. He stared at me incredulously. Takwa laughed nervously and said, nodding in my direction:

'Don't mind him. He thinks because he is a manager from Lagos he can do what he likes in our town.'

Odeh shook his head.

'It's dangerous to go out now, you fool,' he said. 'This is an unofficial curfew. My father's people will clash with Assi's midgets. No one can say what will happen.'

Takwa added:

'Everyone in town knows what it's like.'

I didn't say anything for a while. Takwa opted to stay. If he hadn't taken to mocking me, to reminding Odeh of what I did years ago, and if both of them hadn't ganged up on me and made me feel like an outsider, if they hadn't done all this knowing full well that I was trapped there in Oguso Lodge, I might not have made any decision at all. But I began to think that if the dancers in the streets were dangerous then I must leave. It might have been sheer perversity on my part, but I felt that their cultic activities were no business of mine. Besides, if both cults were clashing how could I be sure I was safe in Odeh's house when the other party might just take to attacking it? After all I was in the home of one of the town's manufacturers of terror. How was I sure I wouldn't be its victim? I had enough of my own problems weighing me down. I decided to leave. I felt up to my neck with our powerful people, our politicians, our governors, who had their cults as a way of maintaining and spreading their influence. I was tired of those who create our realities, and who encircle themselves with dread.

'I'm going,' I said. 'It's good to see you again, Odeh. You have changed.'

He smiled and warned me again that it wasn't sensible to leave. I said my goodbyes, and left.

It was as I traced my way back to the hotel, feeling the curious emptiness of the town, feeling the darkness thicken in the air, remembering my adolescent adventures in those streets, that I became aware of a different aspect of the place that I had forgotten. Years ago we were returning from a football match and we had taken a short cut through the forest when we heard the beating of drums. I heard those drums as I walked down the empty streets. The drums were insistent and eerie. They spoke of dread, of death, of sacrifice. Then I remembered that around that time of year, when the harmattan had passed, and when the rains swelled the river, washed away shacks, and inundated the parched earth, that cults carried out their rituals which seemed a thousand years old. I remembered it had been said that the head of the cult, who was never seen by untitled people, needed blood for his elixir. They said he was one hundred and eighty years old. We who were students lived in fear of returning late to school. We lived in terror of all the stories about the bright students who had vanished, of those that had been killed, their bodies found by the wayside, miles from town. I remembered the dark underbelly of W. And it was with a new fear, a complex adult fear, that I tried to get back to the hotel.

Then suddenly, without any thunderstorms or lightning, it began to rain. The shops were shut along the streets. People looked out furtively from behind their curtains. An occasional car shot down the road. With the rain falling silently, with bells and clanging machetes, drums and cowhorns sounding everywhere, with weird

chants roving the streets disembodied, the town suddenly took on the atmosphere of a place inhabited by
nightmares. All around I could hear the noises of the
rival cults clashing, could hear them engaged in an
eternal battle for power and ascendancy. It has never
been revealed how many heads have been lost in the
encounters. It is the town's secret. The rain poured
down, thunder sounded low in the sky, lightning
flashed over the houses of the poor. And then a woman
ran past me, screaming:

'There are no fish left in the river!'

When I looked round she had disappeared. I began, I
think, to hallucinate. I saw the secrets of the town
dancing in the street: young men with diseases that
melted their faces, beautiful young girls with snakes
coming out of their ears. I saw skeletons dancing with fat
women. I passed the town's graveyard and saw the dead
rising and screaming for children. It seemed as if the
unleashing of ritual forces had released trapped spirits.
Nightmares, riding on two-headed dogs, their faces
worm-eaten, rampaged through the town destroying
cars and buildings. They attacked the roads, they created
pits at the end of streets for unwary drivers to sink into.

It rained harder. I could have sworn that the forests
accelerated in growth and drew closer to the town,
became dark green veils between houses. Floodwater
and rivulets from overflowing gutters swept through the
streets, transferring the garbage from one area to
another. It came as a shock to discover that over certain
houses, which I later identified as belonging to cult
members, the rain did not fall. I pushed on, thoroughly

wet. Thunder clapped above me. I felt the drops of rain beating heavily on my shoulders, as if the rain was composed of stones and not water. Mounds of rubbish, knee-high, formed around me. The lightning flashed, made each second incandescent, and I felt heavy things falling on me, wounding me. And when I looked I saw that it was raining fishes. I screamed. I ran. Children flowed in the water like holographic images, their mouths liverish, their eyes wide open. I noticed that my shirt had been dyed red by the rain. People called out to me several times. When I turned to look for them I saw nothing.

I got to the hotel and found that it was shut. I climbed in through a back window. The hotel was deserted. In the dance-hall there was a white cat sitting on the counter. It stared at me with green eyes. I went upstairs to my room. In the distance, surrounding the town, I heard the thundering drums rolling with the soft pelting of rain. I looked out of the window and was astonished to find that it wasn't raining at all. I went downstairs, through the smelling backyard, and made a proper check. It was raining everywhere, but not over the hotel.

Then I saw a terrible flood-tide rolling down the street, as if a great dam had broken and the tarmac itself had become unleashed. Odeh's father, a crown of money on his head, sat on the crest of water, as if on an invisible barge. His sceptre was of silver. His face was stiffened, as if he were in an advanced stage of demonic possession. Servants, carrying his litter, shouted his praises around him. His cult members, wild and relentless, carried the trophies of the day's victories, the bodies and the spoils of the defeated.

I started to go back in when I noticed that there was a film of dust on the cocoyam plant at the hotel-front. The banana plants were also dry. There was a red moon at the far corner of the sky. Transfixed by all these details, my head turning, I noticed also that the flood-tide had drawn closer. One of the cultists saw me and in an instant, as if to punish me for my impertinence, the thundering drums, the clamour of machetes, came in my direction. I ran into the hotel, barred the door, and tripped over the white cat as I rushed upstairs. When I got to my room the hotel was surrounded with thunder. I sat on the bed, lit a cigarette, and found myself both sweating and trembling. I looked for a bible and found none. I paced up and down the room, not daring to look outside. The cultists hammered at the doors. I heard the sounds of splintering wood. I began frantically to look for something – anything. I ransacked my briefcase. As if I were trapped in a nightmare I looked for something, a magic object, that could save me. A bottle of POWER-DRUG fell on the floor and cracked. The liquid poured out. I heard the door give way downstairs with a mighty crash. In my utter confusion I began to scoop up and drink the contents of the drug that was spilling on the floor. I heard the cultists, who were reputed to eat their glasses after a ritual drink, marching up the stairs. I counted the thunder of their feet. I choked on broken glass. A deafening wail shook the hotel. Then I heard them banging on my door. I opened another bottle of POWER-DRUG. My mouth bled. I had drunk half the bottle when the door caved in and I saw the rush of an undammed river, a flowing black mirror, with lightning flashing all over it. Odeh's father, eyes wide open, was on the crest of the water. Behind him his followers, covered in antimony, held in their hands a miniature of the molue that had crashed into the lagoon. The flood-tide poured over me and I sank into the nightmare of drowning.

The Crude Mythology of Survival

Two days later, Takwa was explaining to me the principles of ritual terror. He said that the imaginings of the victims grab hold of their throats and begin to strangle them. Takwa was in good humour. He told me that the town had witnessed a downpour which would create a new world record. He told me that in some parts of town it had rained blood and that crayfish were seen falling over the market. He said that sections of W. had been virtually rearranged by the tidal rain: that several houses, including a bank and our college chapel, had been washed away altogether. Volunteers had been sent all around the delta area to find the missing buildings. Then he said that as they simply couldn't be found the two millionaires had offered to replace them.

He had come to my room with some other schoolmates and he talked so much I didn't even get a chance to say hello to them.

'How many prostitutes did you have last night?' one of them asked, looking round at the mess of the place.

'None.'

'What have you been doing then?'

I had no idea. I had absolutely no recollection of how I had passed the last two days. I felt as weak as an invalid. My nerves were on edge. I kept trembling. The sound of drums opened up holes in my head. The bats had multiplied in my mind. The clinking of coins, the rustling of pound notes, sent me into a helpless tremor. When Takwa saw the bottles of POWER-DRUG on the floor, he said:

'Ah, he's been keeping a new drug to himself.'

They shared a bottle between them. I protested. They laughed. I began to tell them about the molue beneath the lagoon, of the people who had died, and about the Rastafarian, but they stared at me, swaying. Then they forced my clothes on me and dragged me out to the arena where the financial contest was going to take place. I complained, but I was quite glad to leave the room.

The streets were full of people again. Apart from the overflowing gutters, and the heaps of garbage tangled about the place, it was as if nothing had happened in the town. It might have seemed as if the macabre fiesta had been entirely imagined by me, if I hadn't noticed the scavenging expressions that had crept into people's faces.

Takwa, in an expansive mood, told me that the events of the last three days had been unprecedented. The powers that be, he said, were growing stronger every day. He said that if I wanted to survive in the country, or anywhere in the world, the secret was to join the strongest side and 'pour your blood into the basin'. He said that the forces which rule the country were of a kind impossible to imagine. Takwa sang the praises of the forces, as if they were everywhere, as if they were listening, as if they were a substance of the air that could punish him at any second.

'It's all politics,' he said. 'That's what today's contest is all about.'

'What?'

'Politics,' he said.

'I don't understand.'

'There is no politics without power,' he said. 'And there is no power without fear.'

He looked at me pityingly.

'The strongest fear in this town,' he said, 'is to be defenceless, to be without a powerful godfather, and therefore at the mercy of the drums.'

He rode the wave of his certainty.

'New stars are growing every day. They grow from the same powers, the same rituals . . .'

'. . . the same smell of blood in the afternoon,' I interrupted, paraphrasing Okigbo, the poet.

He shrugged and with a triumphant smile he said:

'That is the beauty of our world.'

I was happy for him. He did not have a sunken molue in his brain. Rastafarians and diseased children didn't torment him. He hadn't been a salesman of nightmares – he had only ever been their administrator. He slapped me on the back. But as we neared the pavilion where the event was gathering momentum his face took on a sneer.

Then he stopped, blocked my path and, to my greatest surprise, asked:

'Whose side are you on?'

My former schoolmates, all of them grounded in that strange town, their faces miserable, their eyes mean and rat-like, their features similar in their despair, crowded me. I stared at Takwa for about three long uncomprehending minutes. Then, at the sound of trumpets from the pavilion, I knew instantly how he kept his job, acquired his expensive habits, his carefree lifestyle, his languid indifference, when everyone else in the town was starving. I also knew that because he was safely on the right side, the strongest side, he would never understand what it was like to live with seven corpses in your dreams, to live with women eaten by ringworm, or children bursting with stomach worms. I spat in Takwa's face and went on to the pavilion. Neither Takwa nor my schoolmates lifted their hands against me. Those were the last two mistakes I made in that town.

When I got to the pavilion I could not see, for there were too many people present. It was an open-air event. At the centre of the gathering there was a covered platform. Around it, packed, sweating, noisy, were the ordinary inhabitants of the town – the touts, beggars, carpenters, bar-owners, prostitutes, managers of pool shops, clerks, oil-rig workers, petty bureaucrats, people with odd afflictions, an old man without an eyelid, a young man with crutches. It was so crowded that it seemed as if the event were a large political rally, or a gathering of people seeking cures from the ministrations of faith-healers. I mingled with the crowd and pushed my way to the front. I heard people around me saying that powerful herbalists were withholding the rain. I could not see. Deep into the crowd, almost unable to move, I realized that I was hungry. I had not eaten, as far as I remembered, for days. The crowd scared me. People kept jostling one another. They were restless and eager for the event to begin. Surrounded by people who looked downtrodden and mean, every face a stranger's, I grew afraid. I felt the POWER-DRUG eating up my stomach, gnawing through the lining, inflaming my intestines.

A mad energy rode me while the proceedings began. I felt angry and reckless. Then as I pushed forward I passed a group of fishermen who had come to the event with nets. They had come to catch money. In a moment of hallucinated illumination it struck me that all those present – the market-women from the creeks of dark rivers, the clerks from remote bureaucracies deep in the delta villages – had one thing in common. We needed modern miracles. We were, all of us, hungry. We had all abandoned our private lives, our business lives, our leisure, our pain, because we wanted to witness miracles. And the miracle we had come to witness, which seemed to comprise the other side of ritual drums and dread, was that of the multiplying currency. We had come to be fed by the great magicians of money, masters of our age.

I still couldn't see. The crowd was so dense that the platform was obscured and only the stars in the sky could be seen, the unnumbered stars, presiding eternally over our curfews and follies.

As I neared the front I heard a voice over the loudspeaker droning on about the unfolding event. I recognized the voice. It belonged to another schoolmate who had become the personal secretary of a politician. When I could see what was going on I was struck with the fact that the platform which seemed so ordinary from the distance was in fact a magnificent dais, a pagoda brightened with coloured lights and golden tinsel. Large portraits of the two millionaires hung on either side of the platform. Odeh, attired in rich brocade, sat at a glass table, fanned by women. Assi sat on the other side. Behind both of them stood the respective bodyguards of their fathers. The ritual dancers associated with both men, dressed in different kinds of animals skins, were far behind. They occasionally clashed their machetes and sent sparks flying in the air.

The contest had begun. The trumpets and the brass sounded. On the foreground of the stage the musicians and praise-singers connected to the two millionaires performed, as if they too were in competition. The man chairing the event came forward and made an announcement. Odeh's father's praise-singers began to shower exaggerated praises on their benefactor. The musicians struck up a tune. A group of female dancers came on. They performed a rain dance, shivering their bottoms. Representatives of the millionaire sprayed money on them.

The crowd became restless. It was announced that Odeh's father had brought an air-conditioned Rolls Royce and that in it he had a large fridge which stored and cooled his money. The people cheered. The fridge

was brought on stage and the stacks of notes were
unloosened from their bindings and thrown at the
crowd. A struggle broke out at the front. Several hands
stretched out and fought for the money. This went on for
a while till a quarter of the fridge's contents were
emptied. The chairman of the event came forward and
made another announcement. The musicians played.
Then suddenly we heard a lowering drone in the air. We
looked up and saw a helicopter circling slowly, just
above us. The helicopter swept off and came back again.
Smoke began to issue from it and we saw a large
glittering banner bearing Assi's father's name and his
portrait. The crowd cheered loudly, hailing the millionaire. The helicopter hovered over us. Then a door
opened and bags of coins were emptied over us. No one
moved for a while. It rained coins through the silence.
We watched the silvery fall, bright in the coloured
spotlights trained on the helicopter. The coins poured on
us, an amazing event. The silvery sparkles floated down
through the air like tangible stars. It was when the coins
fell on us, hurting us, hitting our heads, our faces, that
we began to scramble. The coins rained on us as if it were
our punishment for being below. The coins tinkled on
the roof of the platform. As we struggled bundles of
naira notes were tipped out, and were blown hither and
thither by the propeller blades.

We fought, we climbed on one another, and the crowd
became an area of war. We set upon one another in our
attempts to collect enough money. In spite of having my
arm wrenched, having people tread on my back,
clambering on my neck, and in spite of being punched in

the eye (for my blindness at being there and at joining in), I managed to snatch up a considerable amount of money. The notes were wet. From the stage the chairman hailed the latest spectacle. From the back of the crowd a preacher, with a megaphone, began to denounce the whole event and the entire town:

'For want of vision my people perish!' he quoted.

The chairman made another announcement.

The preacher said:

'It is easier for a camel to pass through . . .'

He never completed his sentence. He was swallowed up by the crowd.

Masquerades came on stage and danced. The praise-singers performed. The musicians played their instruments. The ritual dancers clashed around the pagoda. They brought the fridge on stage again. The helicopter swirled in the air. It went on like that, one spectacle on top of another, leaving us perplexed by the mindless excess and drained of any possibility of wonder. Two hours later, when the crowd were in bruises and tatters, when we had exhausted ourselves fighting for money, the chairman announced Assi's father the winner and declared that the event was over. In a moment the stage was empty. The local celebrities disappeared into their cars. I had not noticed just how many cars, of luxurious varieties, had been parked around the arena. And as they disappeared into the night I nearly missed the fact that I hadn't seen either of the two millionaires.

After the announcement of the winner, the supporters of Odeh's father, screaming that the judges had been bribed, began to rampage. As the local celebrities drove away there was a crackling sound in the sky. Then the lightning flashed, thunder pealed, and it started to rain. The water came down in torrents. The crowd dispersed, surging one way then another. We were the garbage carried away on the waves of mud. The rain brushed us against one another, crowded us past the cemetery, past the marketplace and the cinema.

As I splashed on through the streets, fingering the money I had struggled for, I felt that there was a great hunger, a great rage, amongst us. Everywhere we went that night we saw that the naira notes had fallen over the graves of the dead, over the market stalls, on the huts of the poor, on stationary cars, on heaps of garbage. It was only when I began to pick up the notes on my way to the hotel that I realized we had all been the victims of a cruel prank. When I turned the notes, wet in my hands, the ink began to run. Then I saw that one side of the currencies was authentic, but the other side washed away and became blank. We had been fighting for joke currencies. I remembered what Takwa had said: what side are you on? I began to laugh. I laughed for my wounds, my swollen eye, my wrenched arm. I laughed all the way back to the hotel. As I neared it several women ran past screaming that the cultists had taken to the streets again. In the distance I could hear the preacher shouting:

'Every man to his tent! Every soul to their beds!'

I couldn't care anymore. But when I turned into the street where my hotel was, I suddenly heard Takwa say:

'There he is! Seize him! Seize him quickly! He is an enemy, a spy!'

He had some thugs with him. They came towards me, machetes in their hands, and I ran away and mingled in the crowds dispersing to their various homes. I stayed out in the rain till it was past midnight. The lights went out all over town. I went back to the hotel, climbed in through the back window, and crept upstairs. I hurriedly packed my things and then I went downstairs to pay my bills. Then I took a taxi to the garage and sat under a stall, under the rain, till dawn broke. I caught the first taxi and fled from the town of W. I felt that the meteors of the new curfews blaze for two or three generations. Then afterwards their legacies are scattered by the winds and among the pariah dogs.

Postscript

Three days after I arrived back in Lagos I went to my former offices and learned that CURES UNLIMITED had moved. Their new premises overlooked the lagoon. When I got there the secretary, who looked as if she hadn't eaten since the last time I saw her, told me to go in. My boss stared hard at me. He looked as stocky and as ugly as ever. Then he motioned me to sit down. He chewed on a kola nut, absent-mindedly fanning himself.

'What do you intend to do?' he asked, after a while.

'I have been thinking about it.'

'Your photograph has been in all the newspapers,' he said, smiling, 'so no one will give you a job.'

He paused. Then he asked if I was ready to take my measure as a full-blooded national. I stared at him. I thought about the events in the town of W., about the helicopter, the cultists, and about Takwa's question. I thought about the seven people who had died.

My boss, lashing out with his fan, speaking in an irritated voice, said:

'What's the matter with you, eh? Do you actually hold yourself responsible, eh? Nonsense! Sheer vanity! Those drivers race themselves and have ghastly accidents every other day. Since you've been away three other lorries have driven into the lagoon. They didn't need our medicine to show them the way. Besides, POWER-DRUG has been vastly improved.'

He fetched a bottle and drank a mouthful. Then he slammed the bottle back on the table.

'My boys told me that one of our chemists, who has since been sacked, mistakenly put too much marijuana oil, chloroform, and alcohol into the drug. We have now checked it thoroughly.'

He sat staring at me for a long time. He sat in the same place, fixed, like a statue, as if his brain had been turned to stone. He stayed like that for about five minutes. Then, bellowing suddenly like a bull, he stood up, raged around the office, overturning piles of documents, shouting instructions at his secretary, banging the doors, bristling with a terrible energy. Then after a while he came and sat down. He sweated. His eyes bulged. His face radiated power. He said:

'Are you going to mope around, pitying yourself, or are you going to be a man, an African?'

Through his window I saw the lagoon, green and bright under the sun. Then he told me that my job was still vacant. He offered to increase my salary. I said I would consider it.

When I left the office I thought about what it meant to go back to the molues overcrowded with screaming children and traders. I had to choose. The blank or the authentic. Then, slowly, I began to tease out an understanding of my nightmares. I had to choose if I wanted to be on the block or a buyer, to be protected by power or to be naked, to laugh or to weep. There are few consolations for an honest man, and no one is really sure if this isn't the only chance a poor man has on this planet. I am ashamed to admit it, but I hate suffering. So, resigned to the lengthening curfews, to the lights blinking out in small firmaments, I chose to accept my old job. For a while I took batches of the new POWER-DRUG and made my speeches on buses, by the roadsides, but without my former conviction.

When the new inadequacies of the drug began to manifest themselves again I changed my mind. My boss began to contemplate making medicines to cure the problems that POWER-DRUG created. Where will it end? Like most of our leaders, he creates a problem, then creates another problem to deal with the first one – on and on, endlessly fertile, always creatively spiralling to greater chaos. But it was when I discovered that my boss didn't really use the medicines he manufactured, and after I had saved up enough money, that I decided to quit and attempt to start up my own business.

It was around that time that I learnt of the Rastafarian's survival. In the evenings from the distance, I sometimes heard his odd and poignant voice as he flailed us, saying:

'Africa, we counting on yuh!'

And it was with some sadness that I would turn in the opposite direction and head for the nearest bar. I would order a large calabash of palm-wine and drink to the difficulties of our days. I would drink to the young man who threw himself into the lagoon, blaming his suicide on the government. It was the beginning of the rainy season. My own nightmares had ceased. But I had begun to see our lives as a bit of a nightmare. I think I prefer my former condition.

When the Lights Return

EDE HAD BEEN singing at a poorly attended concert when the power failed. The hotel didn't have any electric generators. The audience shouted for their money to be returned, then they left in disgust. In the darkness Ede saw the luminous white dress of his girlfriend floating up to him. He heard her sad voice say:

'The third time in one night.'

'I don't think they liked my song, Maria.'

She laughed gently.

After a while she said she didn't feel well.

'It's the black-out,' he said absent-mindedly. 'It makes you feel weird at first.'

With the microphone in his hand he stared into the haze of darkness. Her eyes glowed like that of a cat. He put the microphone back on the stand and paid her no further attention. While he joined the musicians in clearing up the instruments she sat in a corner of the stage, feverish in the dark. He didn't notice her again till the hotel manager went around with a lamp and saw her asleep on the floor. Ede woke her up, lifted her into a taxi, and took her home. He was irritated with her that night, and because he was irritated with her he didn't notice that she had begun to change.

He avoided her for a while. He began to think of her as being too soft, too frail, a bit of a spoil-sport. He managed to blame her for the failure of his last concert. He even began to contemplate finding another woman. But when she came to see him, after a week's lack of contact, and after the lights had returned, she looked so beautiful and her eyes were so sad that he forgot all about his petty irritations. Without asking how she was, or whether she was feeling better, he locked the door and began to kiss her. She pushed him away. He held her hands and stared at her. She trembled slightly. Her hands were soft and her palms were damp; beads of sweat glistened under her nose. He made her lie down on the bed. Then he took off her shoes and made her face him.

'I want to watch television,' she said.

'Watch my eyes.'

She smiled. Stealthily, as if he didn't want to disturb her acquiescence, he moved his fingers up her legs. He began to play with her when she sneezed.

'Have you got a cold?'

'I just sneezed.'

'Maybe someone is calling your name.'

'Who?'

'I don't know.'

He went on playing with her warm thighs. She stiffened. He had encountered her wetness. It always

148

came as a surprise.

'You're tickling me.'

He tickled her some more. Then he took off her silk blouse and her skirt and threw them on the armchair. His breathing became laboured. He waited for her protestations.

'What about your mother?' she asked, in a new voice.

Ede lived with his mother in the two small rooms.

'I knew you would bring up something.'

'Well?'

'She's gone to our town people's meeting.'

'So?'

'She'll be gone a long time.'

Maria paused, then asked:

'What if someone comes to visit her?'

'It's okay.'

'What about the door?'

'It's fine.'

She stared at him. Her eyes glowed. When she laughed Ede took a deep breath before burying his face between her breasts.

'It's good to be alive,' he said with a sentimental quaver in his voice.

'Who disputed it?'

'No one.'

They were silent. Gently, she caressed his hair. Then she held onto him with such loving strength that he felt his sudden hardness.

'What if I don't want to?' she said, drawing back a little.

'Then you will be surprised.'

149

'By what?'

'By yourself.'

'Seriously, Ede, what if for no reason I don't want to?'

'What?'

'Seriously.'

'Do you want to kill me?'

'Be serious.'

'Well, I'll be utterly frustra . . .'

Then it happened again, suddenly, without warning, invading their lives. Every day, once, twice, often uncountably, the lights went, plunging everything into darkness, releasing an obsessional tide of heat and sweat and incomprehension.

In the darkness Ede felt the mood change. Maria's body burned beside him. He got up and lit a candle. Maria's face was pale. Her lips trembled. Sweat broke out on her forehead. She had a frightened expression in her eyes. When he started to climb back into bed she pushed him off and got dressed.

'What's the matter?'

'I've got to go.'

'Why?'

'I'm going.'

'Is it because of the light? It'll be back soon.'

'I'm going.'

'Why?'

'Nothing.'

'Why are you so strange all of a sudden?'

'I'm scared.'

'Of what?'

'Nothing.'

He tried to persuade her to stay, but he felt no conviction. Maria's beauty took on a single-minded and uncanny concentration.

'Alright!' he said angrily, 'if you want to go then go!'

Galvanized by the new tone in his voice, she dressed hurriedly. The mosquitoes whined around her. The heat seemed to be rising. If he had looked carefully at her face in the candle-light he would have seen how curiously disturbed she was. But he only noticed what he took to be her indifference. When she was fully dressed she turned her impenetrable eyes to him and said:

'Are you going to see me off?'

Frustrated, unable to understand why she suddenly broke off the mood of the evening, he stayed silent. Holding her head high, she swept up her handbag and left the room. Then he lost his temper, shouting at her incoherently, calling her names. It was very dark in the corridor. Outside, he heard others shouting as well: some at their wives, some at their children, others seemed to shout at the air, as if to register the existence of their protest.

The other voices rose to him, but he drummed on with his insults, hoping that he might get a response out of her, hoping to whip up the sort of confrontation that only an instantaneous reconciliation could resolve. But she didn't rise to his baits. When they passed a stall with kerosene light he saw a shadow on her face, but he didn't recognize it. And when they got to the main road he had aggravated the situation so badly that when a taxi came along all he could do was stare at her threateningly. Before she got into the taxi, she said:

'Don't be bad to me.'

'And why not?'

'Why?'

Without meaning to, without resisting it, irritated by the darkness, he said:

'You're too much trouble. Too frail. Always ill. Too coy. You're not really interested. I don't want to see you again.'

She stared at him. The impatient taxi-driver blasted his horn.

'I don't,' Ede said, with too much feeling, and with some inexplicable satisfaction.

Maria opened the car door and, with the candle-lights reflected in her eyes, said:

'If you do that, if you ignored me and never saw me again, then you would have killed me.'

She looked almost demonic, almost possessed. She continued:

'And if you really love me, and if later you want to talk to me, you would have to wake me up from death. Can you do that?'

Ede didn't understand her. He was quite startled. Without saying another word she disappeared into the taxi. And the taxi, with no back-lights, disappeared into the darkness.

Three weeks passed, and he refused to see her. The black-out had persisted. His mother had kept asking about Maria's absence and he had kept on lying that everything was fine. Then one day, after he had finalized the date of a recording session, and finished a day's work in the office, he had come home bound nerve and brain in exhaustion, when it occurred to him that she was passing completely out of his life. He sat on the armchair, thinking about Maria. He shut his eyes and tried to sleep. The candle flame kept twisting. Mosquitoes whined in his ears. With his eyes shut he saw the candle's shape as an agonized dancer, oily with sweat.

He stank. The mosquitoes and the gnats tormented him. Exhausted from another day's work, flattened by the abnormal efforts of struggling for a bus, dulled by the persistence of the heat waves, he felt as if a hand had wiped clean the slate of his emotions. He gave up the chair and fell asleep on the floor. While he slept he had an unaccountable dream in which Maria stepped out of a mirror. There was an aureole round her head which blinded him momentarily. When he saw her face he was surprised that it had changed to the colour of alabaster. Her eyes were dark holes. Her teeth fell out of her mouth, one by one, as he gazed at her. He woke up suddenly with a sadness like lead in his stomach.

The candle had burned low. He did not feel rested. On the contrary, he felt more drained. He sat up on the floor and could not breathe for the heat. He wished the mosquitoes would spare him for an hour so he might regain the energy he had yielded to the heat, the dust, and the fray. He hoped – and in reality he dared not hope – that the lights would return. He got up and was wiping his face with a towel when he thought he saw Maria at the door. He went out. The corridor was dark and empty. He came back in and resumed sleep. He dreamt again about Maria. She was walking upside-down, in a world of mirrors, naked.

'Why are you walking like that?' he asked.

'Sing for me,' she said.

'Why?'

'Delay what I'm going through.'

'I can't sing till the lights return.'

She laughed. Then he saw her clearly. Flowers grew from her ears. When her head moved he noticed that bats had matted themselves tightly to her hair. He screamed and the bats flew into his eyes. He woke up, soaked in sweat.

'Oh God!' he said, as a queer premonition passed through him.

He got up and lit another candle and blew the old one out. He sat on the chair and wondered how it was that he hadn't seen Maria for three weeks. He felt ashamed of himself. Three weeks! His shame grew so much that he blamed her entirely for the frustrations of the day. He blamed the traffic jams on her. He blamed her for the loss of three shirt buttons during the struggle for buses on his way to work. He managed to blame her for the electric failures.

The candle-flame elongated the scuttling wall-geckos, enlarged the cobwebs. With the heat conquering his consciousness, he decided to go and see Maria, sweating as he was, and to confront her with her handiwork. Releasing himself from his obduracy, Ede got dressed. He left a note for his mother, which read: 'I've gone to see Maria. Will not be long.' He blew out the candle. In the darkness he felt suddenly that his neglect of Maria had gone too far and was now beyond redemption. He left the room key under the doormat, for his mother to find. Then he went through the corridor and out into the compound.

The street had been waiting for him.

In a patch of wasteland, in front of the houses, people were burning piles of rubbish and years of hoarded junk. It was the latest act of desperation. Ede had seen how the long absence of electricity had begun to generate new tensions. The twigs of the fire flared up and brightened the hungry faces of the children. Ede looked over the marshland with its high grasses and its solitary stunted tree. At the edge of the marshland there was a school building whose compound was also used as an abattoir. Ede watched the restless goats that were tied to the school wall. Then he saw that the fire had begun to burn the stunted tree. The animals fought against the ropes. The tree had no leaves and at night he had often seen roosters curled up, asleep, on the bare branches.

Ede passed the fire and the burning tree. The crowd watched the consummation in silence. There were solitary candle-lights at the house fronts, as if the city were keeping vigil. When he got to the main road, to catch a taxi, he saw the city's usual traffic jams. The cars were motionless. Ede waited for an empty taxi. And while he waited he chided himself. What was wrong with him? Who did he think he was? He was fully aware of how fortunate he had been to have met Maria in the first place. He was even more fortunate that she was also interested in him, when there were so many other

musicians and men who out-dazzled him with their
wealth, their success, their status. So why didn't he treat
Maria a little better? Why had he begun to take her so
much for granted? He smiled: he knew. It was the
arrogance and the perversity that comes with small
successes. He had recently brought out his first album,
which was well received, and which was selling well. He
had been interviewed on television and occasionally
someone had recognized him in the streets. But more
than all that, more than the small pleasures of bending
her to his will, he had begun to feel possessed by a new
energy, by the certainty that there are powers in the air,
in the lungs of the transformant, which could clean the
rust out of living, and tune up the spirit's unfettered will.

He waited for fifteen minutes, but the traffic jam didn't
ease. He decided to walk all the way to Maria's place, to
her bungalow sinking in the depths of the Munshin
ghetto. And as he began to walk he had a vision of her
face as it had been three weeks ago: pale and beaded with
sweat along the nose. He found it curious that he was
beginning to remember things about her face which he
hadn't paid attention to at the time. He felt he had done
her a great injustice and was overcome with the exaggerated anxiety that if he didn't hurry she might just start
going out with the first considerate man that came along.

He passed a prophetess who uttered her visions in the
dust-laden street. She carried a placard which read: 'THE
WAGES OF VANITY IS DEATH.' Outside the hut of a
sorcerer two men were in the grip of hallucinations.
There was a white chicken, wildly flapping, in the hands

of one of the men. The two men danced towards Ede, chattering and gnashing their teeth, their raving a kind of invasion. When Ede went past them they sang after him. He crossed the bus-stop and tried to avoid the beggars, who looked as if they had all the world's afflictions septic on their bodies. They were vengeful wraiths who clung to him, dragged at his hands, tugged at his shirt-sleeves, entreating for money. He gave them nothing. He pushed them away and they limped behind him, pleading. On the face of one of the beggar-girls he saw the face of Maria. He saw her as she was one day at the bus-stop when she dipped into the bus fray and emerged screaming, crushed on all sides by the violence of the struggle. She was going home after a visit to his place. He had watched her, amazed that the ferocities of ordinary city existence didn't squash her altogether.

There were cockchaffers in the evening light. The darkness had increased and the inhabitants of the city moved through veils of dust. He passed a crowd of people who stood staring at the road, as if a wondrous and terrible thing were about to happen. He passed children who played hopscotch, surrounded by gutters.

The cockchaffers, weaving in the air, formed clouds over the rubbish heaps along the road. And over the mighty rubbish mound of the market they made such shrill noises that Ede gritted his teeth.

Maria's face came to him again when he got to an intersection where the soldiers were in an electric frenzy. The noise of cars, of human voices, of music from record shops, was quite incredible. It was as if a nameless instrument, whose terrible music is fashioned out of the extremes of human chaos, were being strained to cracking point. The shops, which sold trinkets, bales of cloth, plastic basins, and all manner of artefacts, glittered in the dust of kerosene lamps and the pale orange of electric generators.

He remembered her face when he last made love to her on the settee. She always behaved as if there were something intrinsically wrong about love-making. She had to be endlessly coaxed and she had to be made to feel as if she were not responsible for the act, or for her own enjoyment of it. Strange girl, Ede thought. She always bit her lower lip when she was really enjoying herself. She bit it hard, half-tormented, half-ecstatic.

He came to the hut of a fortune-teller and an interpreter of dreams. He wanted to go in, but he was scared of the visions they might evoke, the requests for spiritual appeasement they might make, if he told them about his dreams.

Further on Ede was surprised to see Maria sleep-walking. He had seen her sleep-walking before, but seeing her in public, crossing the road, frightened him. She seemed completely unmindful of the roaring traffic. He crossed the road after her and he had to run because an articulated lorry shot past, ignoring the soldiers. He pursued her, touched her on the shoulders, and when she turned to face him he could have fainted. It wasn't her. It was a blind woman with milky eyes. Ede staggered away, confused, mumbling. Then he stopped to recover from the shock.

The electric frenzy of the soldiers reached him. They directed the traffic with manic gestures. They stopped cars, flogged drivers, and thrashed motorcyclists on the back. While Ede stood in the midst of the cacophony he heard a tune so familiar that he held his breath. It was his album. He breathed more easily. He listened to his music, blaring out of a record shop, with a smile on his face. He anticipated a phrase, but it never came. The record was cracked and it seemed the record shop owner wasn't around. Hearing his record stuck in a groove annoyed him. He frowned and made an angry gesture. Then he noticed that one of the soldiers directing the traffic had been staring at him with an intense look in his eyes. It struck Ede that he had been absent-mindedly staring at the soldier. He started to move away, but the soldier left off directing the traffic and came over. His whip dangled behind him. When he spoke Ede thought he saw cockchaffers leaping from his mouth.

'Why are you making faces at me, eh?' the soldier asked.

Ede made incoherent noises.

'You don't like the way I do my job, eh?' continued the soldier, his whip dangling.

Ede didn't speak.

'What were you looking at?'

'Me? Nothing.'

'I am a corporal, you know.'

'I know,' Ede said.

'Are you trying to be clever?'

'No.'

'Follow me to the station!'

'Why?'

'I said FOLLOW ME!'

Ede had no real reason to be scared, but the corporal

stared at him, sweating, his eyes red. His uniform stank faintly of urine.

'Why? What have I done?'

'Shut up!' the corporal shouted.

'Why?'

'I say SHUT UP!' the corporal said, spraying Ede's face with spittle.

Ede wiped away the saliva and backed off slowly. A woman came out of a shed and poured a bucketful of slime-water on the road. Car horns clashed in the air. A group of traditional musicians, beating on little drums with their fingers, came towards them. They sang very sadly. When they went past them, Ede – who had often contemplated adapting traditional music for modern purposes – found a possibility for escape. Before he could act the corporal thrashed him on the back.

'STUPID RAT! WHO ARE YOU TO REPLY TO ME WHEN I TALK!' foamed the corporal, lifting the whip again.

Ede didn't wait for a second thrashing. He snatched the whip, pushed the corporal, and ran into the procession of musicians. The corporal slipped on the slimy water and fell. He clawed up some chicken intestines on the road, mistaking them for his whip, and gave chase.

The poor musicians sang of corrupt governments, of bad roads, and of electric failures, when the corporal lashed out at one of their faces with the chicken intestines. Ede, in his attempts to get away, narrowly missed falling into a manhole. He slipped across the road and hid beneath the flyover, where the tethered goats moved restlessly in the darkness.

He smelt urine. Human and animal urine.

The mallams and goatherds were asleep on their mats.

Cloaked in darkness, he watched the musicians shouting at the corporal, pushing him angrily. It was only after the corporal disappeared into the manhole that Ede realized he had witnessed a tiny nemesis. Laughing, he went out through the other side of the flyover. He crossed the road and pushed on. He held his head low, ready, as he passed through the invisible gateway and into the infernal ghetto of Munshin.

Ede found himself continually moving against the flowing crowds of people. Beggars streamed towards him. Groups of praise-singers, who make their living by flattering influential citizens, poured past him. 'I should write a song in praise of Maria,' he thought, as he remembered the first time he went to visit her at the office. Her desk was near the window and it was a hot day. The sun beat mercilessly on her, and yet she remained conscious of her beauty and the difference it made. She was the most challenging woman he had ever met. She always eluded him somehow, as if she were enveloped in a haze, slightly beyond comprehension. It made him hungry to think of her.

He bought some sand-roasted nuts. Two articulated lorries thundered past. The fumes they left behind made him feel sick, unable to breathe; the clouds of dust in the air made him thirsty. He stopped off at a kiosk and bought a bottle of Fanta. The woman selling had a big fleshy face and a frame made massive by the quantity of wrappers she had round her. She talked a lot while he drank. She said the government deliberately created black-outs so that ordinary people would have to bribe officials at the board. He was a quarter-way through the Fanta when she added that it was really because the government despised its own people, that they wanted citizens to walk off into the wild roads, and to disappear into open drains and manholes. Half way through the Fanta, she changed her entire theory. She said the electric failures existed because of the lucrative business in generators.

'Most of the military governors own the companies,' she said, laughing.

The immensity of her body shook with her laughter. A generous face, Ede thought. He laughed as well, infected by her good humour. But then, turning serious, she said:

'It's not a laughing matter.'

He still laughed.

'A child in the compound died because of this.'

He finished the Fanta and paid. She threw his change on the counter.

'I'm sorry to hear that, madam,' he said.

She scowled at him.

'Sorry for yourself.' Then, with an antagonistic expression on her face, she added:

'And who is your madam, eh?'

The kerosene lamp shone on her forehead. Still a generous face, Ede thought as he plunged on through the unending marketplace.

Two vultures circled in the sky. At first he was not sure. He passed the corpse of a grown man on a heap of rubbish beside the road. The body was half-covered with yam peelings and the rotting intestines of cows and goats. People stood around watching the corpse as if it would suddenly get up and do something extraordinary. Ede felt he had seen the dead man before. He wasn't sure. The corporal? It couldn't be. The flies were busy in the half-darkness. Ede pushed through the crowd, picked up a stick, and began to rake off the entrails on the dead man's body. The stench of the rubbish made him feel ill. He was about to pull the body off the heap when he noticed that the dead man's eyes were open. They stared at him. A lizard ran across the dead man's face and suddenly he moved. The crowds of people ran. They fled across the road and overturned stalls in their haste to escape. Ede staggered backwards, with the light of clarity coming and going like a loose connection in his head. The dead man stood up and, fixing Ede with a burning stare, said:

'First they shat on us. Now we shit on ourselves.'

Ede didn't know where to run. The dead man came slowly towards him, bringing an immense variety of smells. Ede moved backwards. The dead man stopped. Then he lifted his right hand up, with one finger pointing at the sky, like a demented preacher, and said, in a voice of monstrous power:

'REVOLT!'

At that moment Ede became aware that the heat was unbearable. The air didn't move. The crowds forced their ways on, pushing past Ede, till he was caught in the stream of confused movements that carried him away from the dead man and his sermon.

The midges came to him in the heat. The wind blew gently. He remembered Maria's depressions. He remembered how she looked when she returned from work, her face worn and crinkled with dust. He remembered when she fell into her curious obsession with death. She began to pore over the obituary notices, commenting on how many pages of the newspapers they took up. She kept drawing his attention to the news stories of accidents on the roads, armed robberies, contract killings, ritual murders, military executions at the beach.

The midges flew into his nose and he had to blow hard into his handkerchief to get them out. He realized, for the first time, how hard it must have been for Maria all along. She used to cry because she could have got a particular job or promotion if only she had less respect for her body. As he approached the bottleneck of a crowd fighting to get through a narrow space ahead, he remembered how odd she became when the lights went. It disturbed him that he was never aware of the precise moment when she started to become afraid of the darkness. Things she had said started to come back to him. How she out-stared a snake in the backyard. How the soldiers would stop buses and commandeer a woman at the slightest whim. How one day, as she was daydreaming in the office, three male-spirits came in through the walls and, with their heads facing backwards, tried to force her to make love to them.

The world wants to eat up her beauty, he thought, as he got to the crowded narrow space. The trouble was caused by a woman's stall. It was the largest for miles around. It had chaotic displays of aluminium buckets, calendars, basins, statuettes, masks and lamps. For people to get past the tight space between stall and road there would have to be some kind of order. But the crowd jostled and struggled. Squashed on all sides, Ede decided that he had suffered enough for one day. He tried to turn and go back home, with the intention of seeing Maria another day, when he realized that going back was worse than going forward. A girl howled in the crowd. Ede fought his way through and emerged with his body drenched in sweat.

Passing a shop that sold imitation ancestral carvings, Ede remembered something strange Maria had said: that a man in the office had sworn to make her his woman, even if it meant using sorcery. Suddenly, as if the confusions of the city were making him hallucinate, he began to see Maria everywhere. He caught her face fleetingly on the faces of old women. He saw her in the eyes of women flashing by on the backs of motorcycles. He thought he saw her from behind, her head and shoulders disappearing into the marketplace.

He went down several crossroads, jumped over gutters to avoid the indifferent truck-pushers, and caught flies in his ears as he listened to the music from the numerous record shops. It occurred to him that when chaos is the god of an era, clamorous music is the deity's chief instrument. He didn't fully understand the thought, but it illuminated why he felt drawn to music that had clear, burning melodic lines like forces of nature. He remembered the last time he went to the beach with Maria.

'Even our seas have gone mad,' she said, referring to the items of sacrifice that had been washed up on the beach like rejected prayers.

'These are new times,' Ede remembered saying. 'We need new skins to cope. New songs.'

'We need new nervous systems,' she had added, laughing.

He heard her laughter through the window. As he hurried on to her room he found his anticipation not only intact, but multiplied by all the obstacles. A wondrous feeling kindled in him at the sound of her. He knocked. A man he had never seen before opened the door.

'Yes, who are you looking for?'

Ede peered into the room. A group of old men and women stood round the bed.

'Maria. Is she in?'

'Who are you?'

'Me?'

'Yes, you.'

The man who had opened the door was cross-eyed and his face was covered in a complicated net of wrinkles.

'My name is Ede . . .'

Then Maria, in a weak voice, called him in. Ede walked into a sorrowful atmosphere. He stood with the people gathered round the bed. Maria, her face paler than ever, was covered up to her neck with a white cloth. She had a red head-tie on. Her eyes were feverish. She looked unbearably lean, her features had arrowed, her eyes were larger. There were the smells of carbolic, incense, and animal sacrifice in the room. The old women kept touching her and mumbling prayers under their breath. The old men looked on with inexplicable sadness in their eyes. A beautiful little girl sat on the bed beside Maria. She had been crying. Maria's eyes kept shutting slowly and opening suddenly. When it looked as if she had fallen asleep the people gathered round her began to leave. The mother of the little girl had to carry her away because she didn't want to leave Maria. Ede could still hear the little girl crying outside. The seven candles fluttered in a corner of the room. Soon Ede was the only person left. He sat down on the bed. Maria opened her eyes wide and said:

'I have been thinking about you.'

Then she shut her eyes again.

'What's wrong?'

'Nothing.'

'What do you mean? Something's wrong.'

'I'm fine.'

There were several bottles of medicine on the table beside her bed. Around the room, as if a herbalist had visited, there were basins of herbal waters with barks and leaves floating in them. There were jujus on all four walls and there was another one on the awning above the door. He had never seen them in Maria's room before.

'I am ashamed and sorry about the way I behaved the last time I saw you.'

The kerosene lamp gave off black smoke. Grotesque shadows stalked the room. Mosquitoes whined. It was hot and stuffy, but Maria did not sweat.

'This mad city has been throwing obstacles in my path, delaying me from reaching you. It took me more than three hours to get here. But how are you, my sweet Maria?'

'I've been looking death in the face,' she said.

'What's been wrong?'

'No one knows. My uncle, the herbalist, thinks I was poisoned or bitten by a snake.'

'A snake? Come on!'

'I don't know. I've been feeling faint. I passed out for two days. I haven't been able to eat, to walk, or do anything. This is the first day I've been able to talk to anyone.'

'Take it easy,' he said, touching her forehead. He felt the boiling heat of her skin.

'They finally sacked me at the office,' she continued. 'I got the letter yesterday, a week after it had been sent. Where have you been all this time?'

'I have been very stupid. I deserve to be punished. I have missed you so much. I'm sorry.'

'Save your sorrow for yourself,' she said, her face brightening. 'I've been throwing up at least twice a day. My head feels like a wizard's drum. What can I do with your sorrow? I might have died while you stayed away.'

'Look, don't be too hard on me.'

'Why not?'

'You don't know how much I've suffered getting here today.'

'So what? I make that journey every day. Every single day. On my way back from work. You're not the only one who suffers, you know.'

Ede looked at her lean face, her shining eyes, and a sudden feeling made him start to cry. She did not hold him or console him. She watched him with bright, pitiless eyes. When he managed to pull himself together he asked:

'How are you feeling now?'

'Fine.'

'I mean really.'

'I'm really fine.'

She had addressed him like a stranger. There was no special affection in her voice. He stared at her. She stared at the ceiling.

'I dreamt that you had died,' he said.

She shivered.

'I haven't yet.'

'I took it to mean that you had stopped loving me.'

'You never know.'

'Have you?'

She shut her eyes. They were silent. Then she said:

'I dreamt that market-women stoned you to death.'

'Don't say such things.'

'And in the dream I had to die for both of us to come back to life.'

'You're frightening me.'

She looked at him as if she had never seen him before.

'Are you strong enough to walk?' he asked, changing the subject.

'Why?'

'It's hot in here. Let's go for some fresh air.'

'Have you got a basin?'

'What for?'

'To catch it in.'

'What?'

'Nothing.'

He watched her for a long moment. Then he drew closer to her. She smiled.

'So long as you don't mind getting what I've got.'

'Come on, Maria.'

He kissed her passionately. She did not respond. Her lips were warm. She shivered again and pushed him away.

'I thought I would never see you again.'

'Impossible.'

'It's only when you want something that I see you anyway.'

'You're wrong,' he said, feeling transparent and ashamed.

'Do you want something to drink?'

'No thanks.'

'I'm a bad host today.'

'Don't worry.'

'In one of my dreams a goat spoke to me with your voice.'

He looked at her, baffled.

'In another dream you sat in a dark room, singing. No one was listening to you except me.'

He sighed.

'Have you written any new songs?'

He wanted to tell her of the song he intended to write in praise of her, but he decided to keep it a secret.

'Yes. I'm writing a song about a burning tree,' he lied. After he had said it he realized that it was a good idea.

'So what about a burning tree?'

'They burnt one near our house.'

'The city is burning.'

'You should have seen the tree.'

'You should have seen what I saw.'

'What?'

'It's nothing.'

He kissed her again.

'Let's go out,' he said.

'I can't go far.'

'Let's go for a short walk.'

While she considered it, he swept the covering off her. She was half-naked underneath. Her stomach had shrunken. His eyes were hungry.

'Do you want to eat up a sick woman?'

He kissed her stomach and smelt the warm herbal essences of her skin. She held his head to her full breasts. He kissed them and she moaned. Then she got out of bed and tied the white sheets round herself. Her bones creaked.

'I sound like an old woman,' she said, laughing.

She brushed her teeth, got dressed, and powdered her face. When she had finished she said:

'I am ready. If I fall you must catch me. I don't want to drown in a gutter.'

He put his arm supportively round her. They went out into the courtyard. In the street, she said:

'The air is bad.'

They passed huts and stalls. She began to talk feverishly, the words moving in and out of focus:

'One night, about three weeks ago, I went out to the

toilet. I saw a man with three heads sitting outside the toilet door. I asked who he was and he spoke to me with your voice. I was scared. When he spoke all of his six eyes shone at me in the dark. Then I heard something hissing. I felt something touch my leg. I ran inside and knocked on people's doors and came back out with a lamp and a knife. But the man had disappeared. I told people what I saw and we searched the compound and we found nothing. When I went to work the next day that man I told you about, who threatened me with sorcery, was sitting on my desk. He left, but whenever he saw me he smiled strangely. When I came back from work that day I fell ill. Just like that. I couldn't sleep unless there was light around. Why didn't you come and see me all this time?'

He had no excuse, except vanity. They walked on. She continued.

'And all this time I've been having strange dreams. Prophets run after me, singing. One-legged visionaries hallucinate around me. I saw strange tall women dressed in black pouring salt out of bags. They poured it out until they had made a white mound. Then they began to scoop the salt back into the bags. When they had done that they tipped it all out again. I saw dead bodies getting out of their graves and walking around the market-places. They bought garri and kola nuts and stared at people. I was at the sea and you were a bird that was flying away. Are you?'

Half afraid, half embarrassed, Ede laughed. The Maria he thought he knew had transformed into something different, had entered into an incomprehensible mist. A

172

curious energy emanated from her face. It was as if the illness had sharpened her spirit.

'I'm dying,' she said.

Ede held her hand.

'Nonsense. Don't talk like that.'

They walked in silence.

'Let's go back,' she said, after a while. 'I am not strong enough.'

They turned and started to go back.

'Why don't you sing for me?'

He did.

He had never sung for anyone in the streets before. He sang of the bicycle-repairer who had crazy dreams of riding on the sea. He sang of friends who died in the Civil War, of mad soldiers and hungry policemen, of children who grow leaner, of buildings in the city that were sinking into the earth. He sang of love, his love for Maria, her love for the world. He got carried away with his improvisations and sang loudly, outdoing the record shops and the bellowing hawkers. She touched him on the arm and said:

'It's alright.'

He sang on. Then she added:

'Or do you think you are Orpheus?'

He stopped singing.

Near the house they encountered Maria's uncle, the herbalist. He had a green feather in his hair and a red cloth round his waist. He had a handsome young boy, an acolyte, with him.

'Go in and rest for your next treatment,' he said sharply to Maria.

They went into the room. Maria got into bed and kept looking at Ede as if she wanted him to be daring. But when he touched her thighs she looked towards the door and said:

'In this heat even the mosquitoes are jealous.'

He lay quietly with her on the bed. He listened to her thinking aloud about getting a new job, living a new life. The heat made him drowsy. He slept for a while, his head on her chest. Her irregular breathing lifted his head and lowered it. Then suddenly she woke him up.

'A spirit entered the room just now. It's been staring at me.'

'Where?'

She pointed in the direction where the seven candles burned in the corner. He saw nothing. He sat up. One of the candles went out.

'Are you tired?' she asked.

'I love you,' he said.

'That's what politicians say to the people.'

'I'm going to stay with you tonight and forever. I will never leave you. And when you are better I would like you to be my wife.'

She giggled and then she fell silent.

'Did you hear me?'

She stayed silent. Then her lips began to quiver. Her limbs trembled. Her eyes opened wide and she stared fixedly ahead of her, at something quite specific but invisible.

'Are you alright?'

Her trembling grew worse. She clung on to him and dug her nails into his arms as she stared straight ahead. The bed began to vibrate. Tears rolled down her face. Ede, worried, shook her. She screamed so piercingly that Ede was momentarily deafened. When he recovered she had got out of bed and was running about the room, cowering against the wall, fighting out against an invisible thing that seemed to bear down on her.

Ede ran over to her, but she ran away from him, as if he had become her antagonist. He caught her, held her, and pinned her down on the floor. She kicked and scratched and fought at him. In an uncanny, guttural voice, she shouted:

'Leave me! Go away! Don't come back!'

She fought wildly and drew blood from his neck. Terrified, Ede called her uncle. When he entered the room she became still. Ede carried her to the bed. She looked pale, her eyes were shut, and she seemed asleep. Her uncle began a preparation of herbal treatment. After a while Maria opened her eyes and stared at Ede sadly.

'Go,' she said. 'I don't want you to see me like this.'

'No, I'm not leaving. I'm staying here tonight.'

'What about your mother? Won't she be worried about you?'

'Just rest,' he said, 'and don't worry about anything.'

There were knocks on the door.

'Go now!'

'No.'

'I will come and see you.'

'When?'

'When I can.'

175

The door opened and Maria's relatives came in. They brought with them an air of mourning. They came into the room and gave Ede rough looks, as if he were intruding, or as if he were in some way responsible for Maria's condition. When they came in he got up from the bed and stood feeling isolated, unwanted. Maria beckoned him. He went over and she said, in a whisper:

'What made you think I would wait for you, anyway?'

'I don't understand.'

'You treat me so badly.'

'Forgive me.'

'You better go before my relatives make you feel unwanted.'

He hovered over her, but she didn't say anything else. Her eyes had become lifeless. He wasn't sure if she had fallen asleep or passed into a coma. Then her lips moved. He leant over.

'I might be yours forever,' she said, weakly.

Then she fell still. He shook her.

'Don't!' her uncle said sternly.

Ede waited, but Maria didn't move.

'It's time for you to go,' her uncle added.

Without knowing what he was doing Ede got up, greeted everyone mechanically, and stumbled out into the courtyard. He passed the handsome young acolyte. As he drew away from Maria's place, confused, he thought he heard her voice ringing in laughter into the yellow dust of the night air.

She's a strange girl, he thought. He passed children playing at street-corners. He took short cuts through the backs of houses and leapt over gutters of stagnant water. She really is a strange girl, he kept thinking as he wound his way back to the main road. A three-headed man outside the toilet? What did she smoke? He smiled as he remembered one morning when he had woken early and had heard a goat being slaughtered at the abattoir opposite their house. At the time he thought a woman was being murdered. He raised an alarm. The compound people had asked him the same question. What did you smoke?

As he came to the crowded marketplace he made out numerous heads floating above the blue haze of dust and darkness. People were still pouring back from their late jobs or visits. Hawkers called out their wares. He heard cries of 'Thief' in the depths of the market. The cries circled the air, shouts followed, then the cries died down. He passed a stall where a man with matted hair was preaching. People around warned one another to watch their pockets, that preachers were often allied with thieves.

Then suddenly a weight of sadness came over Ede. For a moment his eyes clouded and in the ethereal mist Maria came to him, luminous in a white dress. When his eyes cleared he felt different. He felt that something had fallen out of his life. Then he began to see Maria everywhere. She transformed into an owl that was flying away. She became a cat. She turned into a dog that followed him barking. He saw her dark eyes in the eyes of chickens and goats. Dogs looked at him mournfully. He got the curious feeling that she was watching him from all the eyes of the animals, old men, and children.

Beautiful young girls stared at him as if they knew. As he pushed through a crowd he heard a voice far behind him call out:

'Ede! Ede!'

He tried to stop, but the crowd pushed him on. He didn't hear the voice again. Jostled and pushed, wherever he looked he saw, as if in a multiplying mirror, Maria disappearing and passing out of focus. Then he heard something being shouted, being echoed all around the marketplace in a cacophony of ecstatic voices:

'The lights have returned!'

The houses, the stalls with electric bulbs, the shops, all suddenly lit up. It was as if the city had woken from sleep. Ede joined in the cheering. He felt as if a burden had fallen from him. He felt freed from a mysterious pestilence.

At the bottleneck in front of the madam's shop the excitement about the lights turned into commotion. The crowd pushed and struggled, their faces defined in new energies. There was confusion everywhere; people seemed to be running in all directions. After a while Ede realized that the commotion was caused by the movement of cattle being driven towards the corral. He also soon realized that he was trapped between the moving hulks of cattle and the immoveable wall of the crowd. Then he heard someone close by call out:

'Ede! Ede!'

He looked round and saw the handsome acolyte in the crowd, separated from him by the moving cattle. When Ede saw the boy, he knew.

'Maria . . .' the boy shouted, and made a hopeless gesture.

Ede stood confused. He turned and stumbled sideways. He tried to reach the acolyte but he found himself struggling against the grain of the crowd. Someone pushed him. He fell. The crowds, in their hysteria, swept over him. When he got up he felt as if his joints had been wrenched out of their sockets.

'Ede! Ede!' the boy called. 'Stay there. I am coming over.'

But Ede couldn't stand still. He staggered and tripped on the wares of the madam's stall. As he got up he saw Maria standing over him. Then she disappeared and in her place was a midget-girl, with an old body, a young face, and a weird growth of beard. The midget-girl pointed at him and shouted something. She began to jump up and down, pointing excitedly. A moment later Ede heard what she was shouting:

'Djrunk! Djrunk!'

As Ede got up the wares of the stall, the masks, the plates, the trinkets, seemed to cling to his hands.

'Djrunk! Thief!'

The last word went round, and grew in volume. The crowd turned on him. Ede tried to escape, but the market-women caught him and set upon him with sticks and stones. The blood flowed over his face and the lights of the world went out slowly in his eyes. The acolyte arrived too late.

Deep in the marketplace, amid all the cacophony, a woman sang in a voice of agonized sweetness. In Ede's street the electric bulbs swayed in the breeze. The dogs barked at the dust. The wind sighed over the rooftops. Neighbours were quiet, and couples had made up their quarrels. Ede's mother stayed up that night, listening to the frogs croaking all over the marshland.

What the Tapster Saw

THERE WAS ONCE an excellent tapster who enjoyed climbing palm-trees as much as the tapping of their wines. One night he dreamt that while tapping for palm-wine he fell from the tree and died. He was so troubled by the dream that late as it was he went to visit his friend, Tabasco, who was a renowned herbalist. But that night Tabasco was too busy to pay much attention to what the tapster was saying. Harassed by the demands of his many wives, the herbalist kept chewing bundles of alligator pepper seeds and dousing his mouth with palm-wine. When the tapster was about to leave the herbalist drew him aside and, with curious irrelevance, said:

'I used to know a hunter who, one day while hunting, saw a strange antelope. He followed the antelope till it came to an anthill. To his surprise the antelope turned into a woman and then disappeared. The hunter waited near the anthill for the woman to reappear. He fell asleep and when he woke up the ground was full of red water. He looked up and found himself surrounded by nine spirits. He went mad, of course. It took me three weeks to recover after I went inside his head to cure him. A little of his madness entered me. Tomorrow if you bring me three turtles and a big lobe of kola nut I will do something about your dream. But tonight I am very busy.'

The tapster agreed and, disappointed, went back home and drank his way through a gourd of palm-wine. He managed to forget his dream by the time he fell asleep.

In the morning he gathered his ropes and magic potions, tied three empty gourds to his bicycle, and rode out into the forest to begin his day's work. He had been riding for some time when he came to a signboard which read: DELTA OIL COMPANY: THIS AREA IS BEING DRILLED. TRESPASSERS IN DANGER. The tapster stared at the signboard without comprehension. Further along he noticed a strange cluster of palm-trees. He rode through thick cobwebs in order to reach them. The smell of their red-green bark intoxicated him. He immediately tied his magic potions to one of the tree-trunks, brought out his rope, and proceeded to climb. Pressing his feet on both sides of the tree, switching the rope high up the rough rungs of the bark, he pulled himself up rapidly, till his chest began to ache. The morning sun, striking him with an oblique glare, blinded him. As the golden lights exploded in his eyes the branches of the palm-tree receded from him. It was the first time he had fallen in thirty years.

When he woke up he was surprised that he felt no

pain. He even had the curious feeling that the fall had done him some good. He felt unbelievably light and airy. He walked through spangles of glittering cobwebs without the faintest idea of where he was going. Fireflies darted into his nose and ears and re-emerged from his eyes with their lights undimmed. He walked for a long time. Then he saw another signboard which read: DELTA OIL COMPANY: TRESPASSERS WILL BE PERSECUTED. Around him were earth-mounds, grave-stones, a single palm-tree, and flickering mangrove roots. He made a mark on the tree-trunk. Suddenly it became a fully festered wound. As he passed the twisting roots, troubled by the whitish ichors of the wound, they clasped him round the ankles. They held him down and tickled him. When he began to laugh they let him go.

He came to a river, whose water was viscous and didn't seem to move. Near the river there was a borehole. Three turtles lazed on the edge of the borehole, watching him. One of the turtles had Tabasco's face. The tapster was about to say something when a multi-coloured snake emerged from the borehole and slithered past him. When the snake slid into the river the colour of the water changed, and it became transparent and luminous. The snake's skin burned with a roseate flame. While the tapster looked on a voice behind him said:

'Don't turn round.'

The tapster stayed still. The three turtles gazed at him with eyes of glass. Then the turtle that had Tabasco's face urinated in the tapster's direction. The turtle seemed to enjoy the act. The ecstasy on its face made it look positively fiendish. The tapster laughed and a heavy object hit him on the head from behind. He turned round swiftly and saw nothing. He laughed again and was whacked even harder. He felt the substance of his being dissolve. The river seemed to heave during the long silence which followed.

'Where am I?' the tapster asked.

There was another silence. The snake, glittering, slid back out of the river. When the snake passed him it lifted its head and spat at him. The snake went on into the borehole, dazzling with the colours of the sun. The tapster began to tremble. After the trembling ceased a curious serenity spread through him. When he looked around he saw that he had multiplied. He was not sure whether it was his mind or his body which flowed in and out of him.

'Where am I?'

The voice did not answer. Then he heard footsteps moving away. He could not even sleep, for he heard other voices talking over him, talking about him, as if he were not there.

In that world the sun did not set, nor did it rise. It was a single unmoving eye. In the evenings the sun was like a large crystal. In the mornings it was incandescent. The tapster was never allowed to shut his eyes. After a day's wandering, when he lay by the borehole, hallucinating about palm-wine, a foul-smelling creature would come and stuff his eyes with cobwebs. This made his eyes itch and seemed a curious preparation for vision. When the tapster tried to sleep, with his eyes open, he saw the world he knew revolving in red lights. He saw women going to the distant marketplaces, followed by sounds which they didn't hear. He saw that the signboards of the world were getting bigger. He saw the employees of the oil company as they tried to level the forests. When he was hungry another creature, which he couldn't see, would come and feed him a mess of pulped chameleons, millepedes and bark. When he was thirsty the creature gave him a leaking calabash of green liquid. And then later at night another creature, which smelt of rotting agapanthus, crept above him, copulated with him, and left him the grotesque eggs of their nights together.

Then one day he dared to count the eggs. They were seven. He screamed. The river heaved. The snake stuck its head out from the borehole and the laughter of death roared from the sun. The laughter found him, crashed on him, shook him, and left large empty spaces in his head.

That night he fled. Everything fled with him. Then, after a while, he stopped. He abused the place, its terrible inhabitants, its unchanging landscape. Unable to escape, he cursed it ferociously. He was rewarded with several knocks. Then, as the eggs tormented him with the grating noises within them, as if a horrible birth were cranking away inside their monstrous shapes, he learned patience. He learned to watch the sky, and he saw that it wasn't so different from the skies of his drunkenness. He learned not to listen to the birth groaning within the eggs. He also learned that when he kept still everything else around him reflected his stillness.

And then, on another day, the voice came to him and said:

'Everything in your world has endless counterparts in other worlds. There is no shape, no madness, no ecstasy or revolution which does not have its shadow somewhere else. I could tell you stories which would drive you mad. You humans are so slow – you walk two thousand years behind yourselves.'

The voice was soon gone.

Another voice said to him:

'You have been dead for two days. Wake up.'

A creature came and stuffed his eyes with cobwebs. His eyes itched again and he saw that the wars were not yet over. Bombs which had not detonated for freak reasons, and which had lain hidden in farms, suddenly exploded. And some of those who lived as if the original war was over were blown up while they struggled with poverty. He saw the collapse of bridges that were being repaired. He saw roads that spanned wild tracts of forests and malarial swamps, creeks without names, hills without measurements. He saw the mouth of the roads lined with human skeletons, victims of mindless accidents. He saw dogs that followed people up and down the bushpaths and brooding night-tracks. As soon as the dogs vanished they turned into ghommids that swallowed up lonely and unfortified travellers.

Then he saw the unsuccessful attempts to level the forest area and drill for oil. He saw the witch-doctors that had been brought in to drive away the spirits from the forest. They also tried to prevent the torrential rains from falling and attempted to delay the setting of the sun. When all this failed the company hired an expatriate who flew in with explosives left over from the last war. The tapster saw the expatriate plant dynamite round the forest area. After the explosion the tapster saw a thick pall of green smoke. When the smoke cleared the tapster watched a weird spewing up of oil and animal limbs from the ground. The site was eventually abandoned. Agapanthus grew there like blood on a battlefield.

The tapster saw people being shot in coups, in secret executions, in armed robberies. He noticed that those who died were felled by bullets which had their names on them. When his eyes stopped itching the tapster wandered beneath the copper bursts of the sky. He noticed that there were no birds around. Streamers of cobweb membranes weaved over the wounded palm tree.

And then one day, fired by memories of ancient heroes, he pursued a course into the borehole. In the strange environment he saw the multi-coloured snake twisted round a soapstone image. He saw alligators in a lake of bubbling green water. He saw an old man who had died in a sitting position while reading a bible upside-down. Everything seemed on fire, but there was no smoke. Thick slimes of oil seeped down the walls. Roseate flames burned everywhere without consuming any-thing. He heard a noise behind him. He turned and a creature forced a plate containing a messy substance of food into his hands. The creature then indicated that he should eat. The multi-coloured snake uncoiled itself from the soapstone image. While the tapster ate the snake slid over and began to tell him bad jokes. The snake told him stories of how they hang black men in

189

quiet western towns across the great seas, and of how it was possible to strip the skin off a baby without it uttering a sound. The snake laughed. Partly because the snake looked so ridiculous, the tapster laughed as well. Several sharp whacks, as from a steel edge, drummed on his head, and put him out for what could have been aeons of time.

When he recovered he traced his way out of the place. As he passed the man who had died reading the bible upside-down he saw that the man looked exactly like him. He fled from the borehole.

His impatience reached new proportions. He counted the rocks on the ground. He counted the cobwebs, the colours of the sun, the heavings of the river. He counted the number of times the wind blew. He told himself stories. But he found that whatever he told himself that was subversive was simultaneously censored by the knocks. He counted the knocks. He grew used to them.

Then the voice came to him again. It sounded more brutal than usual. The voice said:

'Do you like it here?'

'No.'

The tapster waited for a knock. It didn't arrive.

'Do you want to leave?'

'Yes.'

'What's stopping you?'

'I don't know how.'

The voice was silent.

Another voice said:

'You have been dead for three days.'

The tapster, who had seen the sky and earth from

many angles, who knew the secrets of wine, had learned the most important lesson. He listened without thinking.

'If you want to leave,' the voice said, 'we will have to beat you out.'

'Why?'

'Because you humans only understand pain.'

'We don't.'

There was another pause. He waited for a knock. It came. His thoughts floated around like cobwebs on the wind. The tapster stayed like that, still, through the purple phases of the sun. After a long while the voice said:

'Here are some thoughts to replace the ones that have been knocked away. Do you want to hear them?'

'Yes.'

The voice coughed and began:

'Even the good things in life eventually poison you. There are three kinds of sounds, two kinds of shadows, one gourd for every cracked head, and seven boreholes for those that climb too high. There is an acid in the feel of things. There is a fire which does not burn, but which dissolves the flesh like common salt. The bigger mouth eats the smaller head. The wind blows back to us what we have blown away. There are several ways to burn in your own fire. There is a particular sound which indicates trouble is coming. And your thoughts are merely the footsteps of you tramping round the disaster area of your own mind.'

'Thank you,' the tapster said.

The voice left. The tapster fell asleep.

When he woke up he saw the three turtles lazing again at the edge of the borehole. The turtle with Tabasco's face had on a pair of horn-rimmed glasses and a stethoscope round his neck. The turtles broke a kola nut, divided it amongst themselves, and discussed gravely like scholars without a text. The multi-coloured snake came out of the borehole and made for the river. It paused when it neared the turtles. The tapster was fascinated by its opal eyes.

'There are six moons tonight,' said the turtle with Tabasco's face.

'Yes, there are six moons tonight,' agreed the other turtles.

The snake, lifting up its head, its eyes glittering at the firmament, said:

'There are seven moons tonight.'

The turtles were silent. The snake moved on towards the river. The turtle with Tabasco's face picked up a little rock and threw it at the snake. The other turtles laughed.

'There are no snakes tonight,' said the turtle with Tabasco's face.

As if it were a cue, the other turtles set upon the snake. Tabasco the turtle grabbed it by the neck and began to strangle it with the stethoscope. The other turtles beat its head with rocks. The snake lashed out with its tail. Tabasco and the snake rolled over and fell into the borehole. Noises were heard below. After a while Tabasco the turtle emerged without his glasses and stethoscope. He took up his place amongst the others. They broke another kola nut. Then Tabasco the turtle began to prepare a pipe. Instead of tobacco, he used alligator pepper seeds. He lit the pipe and motioned to the tapster to come closer. The tapster went and sat amongst the turtles on the edge of the borehole. Tabasco the turtle blew black ticklish smoke into the tapster's face and said:

'You have been dead for six days.'

The tapster didn't understand. The turtles gravely resumed their discussions on the numbers of heavenly bodies in the sky.

After some time the smoke had the effect of making the tapster float into a familiar world. A tickling sensation began in his nose. He floated to a moment in his childhood, when his mother carried him on her back on the day of the Masquerades. It was a hot day. The Masquerades thundered past, bellowing plumes of red smoke everywhere so that ordinary mortals would be confused about their awesome ritual aspects. All through that day his nose was on fire. And that night he dreamt that all sorts of mythical figures competed as to who could keep his nose on his face. He re-lived the dream. The mythical figures included the famous blacksmith, who could turn water into metal; the notorious tortoise, with his simple madness for complex situations; and the witch-doctors, who did not have the key to mysteries. As they competed his mother came along, drove them away by scattering a plate full of ground hot pepper, worsening the problem of his nose.

And while the tapster floated in that familiar world the voice came and bore down on him. Another voice said:

'It's getting too late. Wake up.'

Invisible knocks fell on him. It was the most unusual moment of the sun, when it changed from purple to the darkness of the inward eye. After the knocks had stopped the tapster relieved himself of the mighty sneeze which had been gathering. When he sneezed the monstrous eggs exploded, the snake lost its opal eyes, and the voice fissioned into the sounds of several mosquitoes dying for a conversation. Green liquids spewed out from the borehole and blew away the snake, the signboard, and the turtles. When the tapster recovered from the upheaval he looked around. A blue cloud passed before his eyes. Tabasco the herbalist stood over him waving a crude censer, from which issued the most irritating smoke. As soon as their eyes met, Tabasco gave a cry of joy and went to pour a libation on the soapstone image of his shrine. The image had two green glass eyes. At the foot of the shrine there were two turtles in a green basin.

'Where am I?' asked the tapster.

'I'm sorry I didn't pay attention to your dream in the first place,' said the herbalist.

'But where am I?'

'You fell from a palm-tree and you have been dead for seven days. We were going to bury you in the morning. I have been trying to reach you all this time. I won't charge you for my services; in fact I'd rather pay you, because all these years as a herbalist I have never had a more interesting case, nor a better conversation.'

London, June 1987